That's Not Me

National Suicide Prevention Lifeline
1-800-273-8255

Crisis Text Line
Text HOME
to 741741

To my Mom and mothers that are full of life.
To my Dad and fathers that are full of fun.
To Aaron and friendships that will always be.

Introduction

Palo Duro Canyon is the second largest canyon in the United States. I grew up only thirty minutes away from its sprawling cliffs, and although vastly beautiful, it never felt like something that big. I had seen it various times when I was little, but while growing up, it remained a place sitting on the back-burner of my mind as I never gave it a second thought.

In my mid-twenties I became a man who attempted to be something he wasn't. I tried being the party-ready guy who drank heavily and slept each day until noon. I tried the relationship path. I tried finding the elusive "one" I grew up hearing about. I did meet someone who was probably pretty close to filling that empty spot. At that time, I found myself crashing into a world of depression, anxiety, and suicidal thoughts. After our breakup, I found someone to comfort me and to help explore my sexuality in new ways. This exploration proved to be a temporary fix to my depression, and I started waking up early and rediscovered the canyon again, waiting for me to explore.

As a twenty-six-year-old janitor I could be found hiking various trails and climbing up cliffs to see what was on top. In these moments I began to appreciate the vastness of the canyon. It isn't deep like the Grand Canyon, but it is huge and spread out. To me, the canyon felt unregulated and wild with no guard rails making it easy to wander off the trails. It was exactly where I wanted to be.

Frequently, I told myself that the dangers of the canyon were why I explored. I could learn to trust myself again here.

It was a place where my depression and anxiety would have to come to die. To my dismay though, it wasn't that simple. I still felt that overwhelming weight of anxiety on my chest. I still felt that heaviness I drug around as depression clouded my mind. I felt the enticing comfort of suicide creeping back into my inner thoughts.

I never told anyone when I would go to the canyon, and I especially never told them where I would be hiking. My best friend would ask me on a daily basis if I had made my way out to the canyon at any time. I would fill him in about the times I almost fell to my death or found a cave that was too small for me to crawl through. We would laugh together about these times as I overenthusiastically explained the dangers I would put myself through. My parents would not approve of the lifestyle I was living even though they encouraged me to get out of my small one bedroom apartment from time to time.

As I laughed with my friend, I saw the real reason I took such risks at the canyon. The risk of going off trail and being lost, the risk of laying on my stomach and pushing myself through a small cave reaching as far inside the canyon as possible and getting stuck. Also, the risk of standing on the side of a cliff and losing my footing to fall a hundred feet to my death actually beckoned to me. I found out there, just below my smile and laughter, sat a deep urge for something to actually go wrong when I did these things. I was hoping that something would happen so people could blame my death on an accident without knowing the dark thoughts of suicide that penetrated my head.

As I hiked, I would think about what would happen after I slipped, fell, and hit a rock killing me instantly. I would envision my parents knowing an accident had occurred and nothing more. I imagined my best friend wondering if my depression had been the cause of the fall, but ultimately, his mind would be at peace knowing that sometimes accidents happen. These thoughts progressed into thoughts about the reaction of my friends and family if I actually did commit suicide. How would the people I love react to knowing I had taken my own life? I thought about various cinematic ways I could do it, ways that would create the most impact. There was a grotesque darkness in my head that became a familiar comforting place. Imagining my friends and family care so much about me gave a deceptive comfort. I would dive deeply into these thoughts and forget that if I actually did go through with it, I wouldn't be around to ever feel these thoughts. They were realities I would never get to experience.

The thoughts frequently came as I hiked. I never thought about why I shouldn't go through with it, but I also never thought about why I should go through with it. I was stuck inside my own head watching thoughts I would never truly think and feeling things I would never truly feel. Caught up in my inescapable depression and anxiety, I came to the ultimate conclusion to end my own life. I decided that I could hike to my favorite spot and use a gun. I would be found at the top of a cliff overlooking the canyon. My last view would be the canyon's beauty but with a gun held loosely in my lifeless hand.

Late one night, I wrote a suicide letter and addressed it to "everyone." This letter wasn't filled with memories or comforting words to my loved ones. It was filled with anger, hate, and worst of all, it was filled with apathy. I have written excerpts from that letter in this book. In order to reveal how my own mind was operating and how deeply disturbed I came to be. I want to reveal how I put the blame on everyone else. It was me in the dark recesses of my mind trying to justify my actions. Later, I went to the canyon again and hiked to my favorite spot. It had a wide view of the canyon. It was hard to find, and it was beautiful to watch the sun spring to life with color there. It was in this place that I pulled out my phone and opened the notes application. I typed out the words "this is where I killed myself." I sat looking at those six words for a moment. My thoughts began to spin, but not as I had expected. I didn't think about killing myself. I thought of a fictional character that had already killed himself. I continued typing furiously, curious to see the story unfold.

Instead of thinking about how to kill *myself*, I was thinking about the life of a person who had already killed *himself*. I wasn't thinking about the success or failure of the story or even how long it would take to complete. I didn't think about how it would be a book or hope at that time that it would be anything to help anyone. It was simply a story that, unbeknownst to me, was saving my life.

I would write rough drafts at the canyon then drive to Palace Coffee, a local coffee shop in Amarillo. Sometimes, I would be there when the doors opened and leave when they closed. The story unfolded rapidly, I only took breaks to go to the restroom or to order another large hot chocolate with no whipped cream (Palace has the best hot chocolate, hands down). One day, I looked down and saw the word count of my story had jumped from the six beginning words to around thirty three thousand.

I had written a book. I couldn't believe it. I was a common man with no accomplishments except for mistakes, and here I sat with a book I had written. A year later, it had been edited and was now ready to publish. I began writing more stories as this old, forgotten passion to write pushed its way to the surface of my life. In the darkest place of my life up until that point, where in sorrow and self-pity I had been so close to ending it, I rediscovered my passion and goal. It wasn't a light. No, I found that later, but I had found my goal. I had found an alternate destination.

I'm not saying these words could fix anyone's depression or anxiety. I cannot stress enough the importance of seeking professional help if you are in a dark place. Find a counselor or therapist that works for you. Reach out to friends and family who want to see you thrive. If you don't struggle with these feelings but know someone who does, reach out to them! The importance of reaching out cannot be overemphasized! Text that person right now and make plans. Regardless of his or her reaction, be the person they need in their life.

We need you. You are important. This book was written specifically for you. Pick up a pen and paper and start writing. I'm not saying what I did is a fix for everyone. What I will say is that writing my thoughts down is calming for me, and maybe it will prove to be helpful to someone out there as well. Writing takes thoughts from the darkness of our minds into the light of day.

Make it terrible. Make it the worst thing you've ever written, and then write some more. Write how you feel. Write a story. Write something that begins in the back of your mind and ends on pages filled with loose thoughts of grammatically incorrect insanity. Get every good and awful thought swinging around in your head onto paper and clear your mind. Show everyone, or don't show anyone. It doesn't matter. What matters is you.

I hope you get something out of this book even though it is just a work of fiction. Writing it cleared my head several times and gave me the desire to continue. I hope that the book helps you in one way or another. You will notice that the protagonists of the book do not have names. The lack of names was deliberate.

That's Not Me

Daniel Chambers

1

"This is where I killed myself," he said solemnly.

She barely made out the comment as she stuffed her half empty bottle of water into her backpack. The small, purple bag zipped up smoothly as she placed it on the ground. She watched him as he stood on the edge of the large cliff they had just hiked. The route was all too familiar to them both, as they had trekked it many times before. Before, when they were both caught up in moments of euphoric bliss. Before, when every day was a new adventure and nothing stood in their way. Those times were gone now, leaving faded memories that sprung back so quickly with a simple—yet long overdue—phone call.

The man perched on the precipice in front of her, a long-lost friend from another chapter of her life, was as mysterious as the reason he had contacted her in the first place. She now lived her normal life with a boyfriend she cherished and adored. Five years had passed since she had heard anything from the man who stood now a stone's throw away from her. Five years of complete silence followed by a sudden phone call was enough to cause anyone to second guess the comment he made. She forced his comment to the back of her mind, choosing to only be happy standing in the early dawn with him.

She reminisced about the bond they once had; how energizing it had felt in the beginning. After a swift mutual connection due to common interests and the same sarcastic sense of humor, things quickly turned toward the intimate and sexual. She couldn't think of anyone she felt more comfortable with sharing those types of intimate moments. The anticipation of spending time with him had kicked into overdrive as they quickly became lovers. Waking up to him shirtless, cooking an early breakfast and rain lightly tapping on the window, was something she could get used to. His companionship provided refuge from the world she so desperately wanted to forget.

Though everything seemed nearly perfect on paper, something held her back. She couldn't quite put her finger on it, but when she thought about the person she wanted to be with forever, it was never him. The powerful spark she desired to feel for him was merely a flicker. She loved him deeply, but was not in love with him. She hated even thinking that old outdated cliché, but sometimes clichés were true. Over time, it became clear that he wanted more than she could give. It wasn't as if she had hidden those feelings from him, but still she felt incredibly guilty. She had been truthful and transparent from the start. She didn't plan to be with him for the long haul. That was the original agreement, that was the original plan. Then it all changed.

In the beginning, they often joked about not developing actual feelings that could ruin their carefree friendship together. They were not supposed to fall in love with each other. So when he started to push her about what it was they were to each other, she was overwhelmed with confusion and frustration. It somehow became her fault that he developed romantic feelings and she didn't. The friction between them heightened as he began to imply that she had never really cared about him and was only using him. What happened to their friendship? To their agreement? "Friends with benefits," as they say. That's what they were supposed to be. That's what *he* agreed to. Finally, it became too painful for him to continue the friendship if she couldn't commit to him. So, he left. She tried not to blame him. He couldn't change his feelings and she wouldn't change hers. It was a clean break. Until today they had no contact so they could both heal. Without the clichéd "we can still be friends" that accompanied most breakups; she was left with a gaping hole.

Watching him now, she studied the man that she had been through so much with. She no longer felt any physical desire for him like she once had; although, even without feeling attraction she still recognized him as handsome. He wasn't an incredibly strong individual, but was nicely toned and tall. He had a jaw line that could cut glass and eyes that would give you a lasting embrace with just a simple glance. She felt a warmth thinking about how things had finally come full circle. She couldn't believe that after all this time they were both able to return to this cliff where they had shared so many memories. On multiple occasions, this place provided the backdrop for relaxing after a long week, or for sorting out a stressful period of life.

She turned her head and saw a couple of black spots burnt onto the rock where they stood. On the Fourth of July, she remembered lighting sparklers here with him when she had no family to spend the day with. He had escaped his own family gathering to spend the holiday with her by telling them he was terribly sick. She remembered the firecrackers they lit just to watch the small explosions. These left the deep scars on the canyon's cliff she saw now; a small mark of ownership from him and her. It was something he did for her to remind her that she could be a child even today as an adult. Her childhood experience wasn't what anyone would consider healthy, but knowing she could lean on him provided comfort enough. No friend had ever cared for her like he did.

The canyon sat roughly an hour away from the city where they both lived; yet, she had never ventured out there after they separated. Over the five years before his unexpected invitation, she had wanted to go back, but felt that this cliff belonged exclusively to him and her as a pair. She missed it—the long hike to get to this spot, the small pond and cabin they passed along the way, and how only brave and adventurous souls would climb over the large boulders to be rewarded by the cliff's beautiful view. She missed the light breeze she could feel as the sun slowly ascended into the blue sky. Looking behind her, she could just barely see the top of the cabin over the boulders. Standing by the cabin, only a sliver of the cliff was visible if you only happened to notice it or knew it was there already. She missed everything about this spot.

She wanted so badly for this to be the beginning of something new and good for them both. The rekindling of a dear friendship. Did she remember feeling this during the call, or was it a desire that popped into her head as they were hiking up memory lane? She guessed it didn't matter either way. They had shared so much, and shouldn't need to remain completely removed from each other.

She had worried about how her current boyfriend would react to her desire to see a friend from ages ago, especially one she had been physically involved with. She fumbled over her words as she told her boyfriend about the reunion, but to her delight, he showed nothing but complete trust in her. Of course, she would have gone with or without her boyfriend's permission, but it bolstered her confidence in their relationship to feel such a level of trust with seemingly no repercussions. She hated any type of conflict and shut down in the face of it. However, with this security, she felt completely at ease to spend time with this friend from her past.

The conflict she now feared; however, was not related to her boyfriend, but to the ominous comment she heard upon reaching the top of the cliff. *This is where I killed myself?* Though she had attempted to distract herself, his words echoed in her ears and gnawed at her consciousness, making her feel uneasy. Why did he bring her here and say something like that? Was he trying to demonstrate how much she hurt him? Attempting to guilt her into rekindling their relationship?

Upon this realization, she was flooded with reminders of why she couldn't handle being together with him. He had always tried to pull stunts like this, making him come off as desperate and untrustworthy. A bait and switch that always resulted in a manipulative friend only seeking what he wants, not thinking of the people he could hurt. They could be laughing and having a great time, then he would sabotage it by overthinking everything, becoming irrational, or making inflammatory comments. Time is a funny thing, she thought. It magnifies the good memories while blurring the bad. It tricked her into accepting his call in the first place. The situation she now found herself in was the fault of time's idealistic recollections, a dash of curiosity, plus a little of her own weak will.

When he called her, she should have just ignored it and gone on with her life. Her current relationship was thriving. Why did she answer his call? She now found herself standing on the edge of a cliff, feeling the palpable tension of the comment he made. This is where he killed himself? What could this remark possibly add to this moment? What is he trying to accomplish?

"What was that?" she asked him, turning back to see him still watching the light pour into the canyon as morning filled the air. She knew what he had said, but prayed she had somehow misheard it.

Turning away from the canyon, he surveyed her, sweaty, bruised, and out of breath from the hike. The beauty of nature didn't compare to what he saw in her. He wanted to smile thinking about how much he missed her, but could only feel distressed by the weight of the impending conversation they were about to have.

"This is where I killed myself," he repeated, deliberately not breaking eye contact. He attempted to portray a sense of control and sound mind; something he knew she would have neither of in the coming talk. Taking a deep breath of agitation, she fixed her eyes downward at her backpack. She tried to make sense of what she heard; she wanted nothing more than to grab her bag and scramble back to civilization.

"So, what does that mean?" she demanded, desperately hoping to evade a serious conversation today. Nothing could erase the warmth of her memories faster than him dredging up old practices. After all this time, she was sure things would be different, but she was starting to realize that he really hadn't changed at all.

His eyes left hers as he walked toward a bush growing behind them. He approached it's cracked, dry, broken leaves, which had clearly been dead for quite some time. The bush butted up against a large rock that provided a spot where someone could easily take a rest. Standing opposite the bush, just out of her line of sight, he gestured with his finger toward something on the ground. Her eyes tentatively followed the direction of his signal. She desperately hoped the discovery at what was on the ground would somehow end in laughter and amusement. She stared down at the ground where his finger pointed. She gasped at the sight. Her mouth now agape as she stood staring at a large, dark red stain that covered the rocky ground beside the bush. She wanted to believe it was dried paint, but knew better. Grabbing her open mouth, she stumbled backward shaking. The atmosphere of the canyon suddenly shifted. The good and bad memories she had now seemed trivial to the stain of red staring at her. Something dark had occurred here and he was somehow involved.

"What...is that?" she squeaked breathlessly. His hand lowered to his side as he stared at the red. He knew this would be very difficult for her to comprehend.

He moved back to allow her a better view, "I think you already know what it is."

She studied the stain—a giant oval spread across the porous rock. She didn't want to get any closer if it was, in fact, what she thought it was.

"To be fair, you wouldn't know about what happened, I guess. I think it's been five years since we've talked? So no, nobody would have told you about it."

She did not need the reminder; he was right. She hadn't forgotten the five long years without him in her life. It wasn't just him that the parting crushed, it was her also. The months that followed the break weighed heavily on her heart. At the time, the only escape from the agony of losing her best friend was to plunge deeper into the rabbit hole of her childhood pain.

During her time alone, she thought a lot about the moment her mother died. A moment she kept buried away deep inside her, letting it manifest into depression and anxiety that he was supposed to help subdue. The feeling of him leaving stung heavily, but paled in comparison to losing her mother at such a young age. The hurt of losing a loved one that lived on was not comparable to losing someone she would never get back. Her preoccupation with her mother's demise, coupled with his pledge not to contact her, eventually allowed her to push the feelings about their dissolved relationship into the recesses of her mind. This begged the question—why did he break the promise and call her now?

Over the phone he told her that his life had completely changed. As she pulled into the driveway to pick him up, she could instantly perceive something had been different about him. He had lost weight, looked well-groomed, and had a calm, mature demeanor about him. As he sat in the passenger seat and spoke to her, his voice was strong and confident. She turned down her acoustic indie music and detected a gleam of hope and excitement radiating from his pupils. Driving to the canyon, she mentally noted that he joked a lot more than she remembered. He appeared to have no cares in the world and it felt like it did way back in the beginning. She chuckled at his jokes, but mostly smiled at how nice it was to see him living his best life and loving every minute of it.

In an instant, they were getting out of the car to hike to the cliff, she could see the eagerness in his eyes for her to visit the canyon again. The hike felt exactly the same as they passed the small pond and eventually the cabin. They laughed about old times. It was exactly how she wanted it to be, up until now. The odd comment about suicide and the red stain felt almost like a curse he placed over the day. What was this? Had he been pondering and planning for five years on how he could win her back?

"I'm telling the truth," his voice pierced through her wall of thoughts as he leaned against the large rock sitting on the other side of the stain. Her thoughts halted as she turned to look at him. The brightness she had seen in his eyes had faded away. All that she saw now was a cowardly version of a man she once knew who couldn't move on from something that would never happen.

"You're not," she rolled her eyes disapprovingly. She turned away from him with a false sense of apathy towards the conversation. His body was still propped up against the giant rock, arms hanging relaxed at his sides.

"Is this why you brought me out here? To guilt trip me into wanting to be with you?" she questioned, feeling betrayed. He snickered at her response as her face warped into confusion. Laughter? Was she wrong? If it wasn't him trying to rekindle their relationship, then what was it?

"I knew you'd probably assume something like that," he responded, curtailing his laughter. Ignoring her obvious pleas to indulge her theories of why they were there, he stared out into the distant canyon. He watched the sun slowly make its way above the line where the earth and sky met.

"It's beautiful out here," he took a deep breath, as if trying to ingest as much of the canyon air as possible. She impatiently awaited the explanation for the hoax he had concocted. He swallowed hard and chose his words carefully.

"After we parted ways, I spent a lot of time coming to this spot, standing right there on the edge of this cliff—our cliff," he said as he pointed to the edge. Resentment crept into her heart as he implied she had forgotten the memories they shared there. Choosing his words deliberately would prove to be the right move for this delicate exchange. He knew having a conversation with her always operated like a chess match. One wrong move and it would turn the entire conversation upside down. Unbeknownst to her, he was about to change the game.

"It...it always gave me the same feeling I used to get when I stood near you. The feeling of weightlessness. The feeling of sudden adrenaline pumping through my veins as I stared at that beautiful sunrise over the canyon." His eyes glistened at the soft morning reflection. She groaned at his romantic comment. To her, these words came across as nothing more than a desperate ploy to stir up old feelings. He knew that this couldn't be further from the truth. She glanced down at the red stain and back up to him; she tried to convince herself this was going nowhere. She walked to her backpack and hoisted it onto her back.

"How charming" she rolled her eyes, then fixed them back to him. "So, what? We come out here so you can confess your love and we're supposed to live happily ever after? You're a piece of work. I have a boyfriend now."

He leaned back against the boulder, resting his hands on the back of his head. He really did not expect her to try to run away from this so soon. Most people would at least have been intrigued enough to hear him out, but she was not like most people.

"We didn't come out here for that," he closed his eyes, relaxed and unfazed by her attempt to leave. She tightened the straps around her shoulders, still barely paying attention to his words. She couldn't start this with him again.

"I know you don't believe me. Take your phone out and check my Facebook," he calmly requested before she left.

She stopped fidgeting with her backpack and stared at him, annoyed. What did he have to prove; that he killed himself? Him lying on the boulder talking to her was evidence enough that he hadn't. Him speaking in riddles and being evasive didn't convey truth either. It only further demonstrated that he enjoyed manipulating the conversation for his own benefit. Still, curiosity was a terrible thing to a tormented mind.

"Alright, I'll humor you." She loosened her backpack and placed it on the ground. Her phone sat in the side pocket, she pulled it out, turned it on, and tapped the Facebook icon. The last perk that sealed their affinity for that particular spot was the phone service. The only place in the canyon that had any reception. They had often watched Netflix or YouTube videos when they were up there. They spent nights under the stars watching "Sherlock" for the hundredth time. Some people might have considered this disrespectful to the beauty of the surrounding nature, but they would joke that those people ought to mind their own business.

She went to unblock his profile so she could view it once again. She recalled for a moment how difficult it was to block him in the first place, and how simple it felt to unblock him now. There he was, an old picture of him smiling, holding a beer and cigarette that she had taken on her couch. She considered this absolute proof that he was not over her. She quickly scrolled down his wall and was met with puzzling comments.

"I'm so sorry...," read the first comment from someone she didn't recognize. A person he most likely met after they parted. When they had been close, she had known everyone in his life, and he knew everyone in hers. The second comment made her heart pound up her throat.

"I still can't believe this. I miss you," from a friend of his that lived out of town. He often talked about how they were close until he moved away. This comment especially moved her, considering that she had heard this friend had a masculinity complex and always shied away from showing emotions. The fact that he even typed those words spoke volumes about how much he was affected. Her mind was whirling. What did this mean? She continued scrolling.

"I don't know what to write. I still can't fathom that you're gone. I still can't see clearly. I wake up thinking about you and I go to sleep wondering what I did wrong. I see your Facebook and want to break my computer. There are so many things I would have done differently. I miss you. I love you," written by his dad.

The phone dropped out of her hand and bounced on the dirt below. She remained motionless; her vision blurred from the tears filling her eyes. She covered her nose and mouth as tears burned her eyes. She knew his dad and couldn't fathom the pain of him losing his son. Her eyes shifted to him lying on the boulder without a care in the world. He breathed in slowly and deliberately. He looked calm and collected, his body relaxed. He seemed to enjoy the warm morning atmosphere that was over-taking the night air. She rubbed her eyes in disbelief and looked at him again. Was she talking to a dead man? The body on the boulder looked very much alive.

She had to remain calm if she sought to find answers. This proved difficult since her eyes wanted to burst like a dam and her vocal chords wanted to scream for help. There must be a reasonable explanation for this. She thought that he must have logged into those other profiles and posted the comments himself, all part of his intricate ruse. After all, five years was a lot of time to plan. Would he really go that far though? Whatever this was remained a mystery and felt unreal.

She slipped her phone into her backpack, hands shaking, and pulled out her half empty bottle of water. She brought the bottle to her mouth and whispered to herself.

"I really wish you were vodka right now," but to her dis-appointment, the water refreshed her throat, and didn't alter her mind. She took a deep breath to regain her composure, and re-turned with an unsteady gait to where he lay. His eyes remained shut, but her comment cracked a grin across his face.

"It sounds like you checked my Facebook. I never thought I'd see Travis say he missed me. That was especially nice," he spoke calmly and relaxed as if discussing the day's weather.

Her mouth gaped open in surprise. She thought about

her next words; her next move on the hypothetical chess board. "So then, what now? Why are you here? For that matter, how did you get here?"

His eyes popped open and he lifted himself to look at her. He appeared excited and ready. "Finally, we can get to some real conversation." Pushing himself off the boulder, he brushed the dust off his jeans. He walked to her backpack and pulled out his water bottle, taking a swig. "I know why I'm here, but I don't really know how I got here," he replied, holding the bottle loosely between his fingers.

She crossed her arms in defense, noticing they were getting warm and probably sunburned. "Well, were you in heaven? Hell? Meet the big man himself?" She was upset by the fact that if he were telling the truth he hadn't already mentioned these things up front.

He knew she would be desperate for this information. Questions about the afterlife had haunted her since her mother died, and together they had mulled it over time and time again. This only reinforced the idea that this was a scheme of sorts, and she had not yet figured out his angle.

"That's one thing I know I can't talk about. Anything to do with what's after death. Mum's the word." Using his hand, he did an imaginary lock and key motion on his closed lips. She uncrossed her arms and reached in her bag, pulling out her sunscreen.

"Well isn't that convenient," she said as she uncapped the bottle and sprayed her arms and legs before asking if he wanted any.

"I really don't need any, but thanks," he lifted his hand in polite refusal. She rolled her eyes, knowing he declined because he was pretending to be dead and didn't need it. She tried her best to seem as uninterested as possible, especially with the continuing mounting evidence that he was a liar and manipulator. She did not want to give him the satisfaction.

"What I do remember is putting the gun to my head. Everything went black after that." These words did catch her attention. She put the sunscreen back into her bag with the water bottles and stood up straight, hoping to learn more about this so-called suicidal experience. It wasn't every day that someone heard a firsthand account of a successful suicide. He turned slightly and stared into the distance.

"I had this heaviness on my chest that I could never get rid of. Then, as I sat there looking at the sunrise, everything went numb. It wasn't like I was even making a decision. It was like the decision had already been made and I was merely carrying out the assignment. With the gun against my head, the horizon in front of me, everything went black as if I had closed my eyes— but I hadn't. Instantly I had overwhelming knowledge. Things I didn't even know I could comprehend were now clear to me. It felt like my mind was always missing several pieces of a puzzle and, suddenly, everything was filled in. I discovered interesting things about the world, my friends and family, and even you."

As he looked back to her, she turned away once again to appear unengaged. She casually plucked dead leaves off the bush next to her.

"Yeah? What did you learn about me?" she asked halfway interested.

He gazed down at the ground trying to find the words. Holding the bottle tightly against his chest with both hands, he closed his eyes, forcing the words to come out.

"I learned that you're planning to kill yourself," he said matter-of-factly.

She stopped picking leaves as her mind digested the words that flowed through her ears. She stared directly into the bush, through the dry branches, through the dead leaves barely holding on, to where the stain could barely be seen on the other side. She felt faint. How could he...? Her dark secret was dragged into broad daylight by a person who calmly and unceremoniously saw deep into her soul. She panicked, frantically searching her mind for a response. There were no more hidden chess strategies. He had just capsized the board and scattered her game pieces. In that moment, he had snatched her from her comfort zone, like ripping off a bandage to expose a wound. Her mind went into an anxiety-filled defense. She wasn't worried about whether it was true or not—it absolutely was. She thought about suicide often. How she would do it? Where she would do it? But, him having information like that felt impossible unless what he said was true. She was talking to a dead man.

2

"That isn't true. I've never thought about suicide. I'm happy," her mouth trembled as she snapped back at him. She tensed up in defense, arms crossed, and squeezed tightly against her body. She felt queasy over the direction this conversation was now heading. Still, she was certain he had no proof. If she could just stop her body from trembling, she could deny everything. He couldn't continue this accusation without evidence, and he obviously had none.

She kept those feelings securely guarded from everyone. Nobody knew that lurking just below the surface of her every thought was the nagging desire to end it all. The darkness would build itself up higher and higher in her consciousness until she could no longer ignore it. She would contemplate where and how she would do it. Would she use a gun? A razor? She could hang herself from a tree. Something slow might be preferable. That way she could dramatically replay scenes from her life like a movie in her head before it all went black. However, something quick wouldn't allow her to lose her nerve and back out. She could pull a trigger and it would all be over in an instant. No, slow would be better...maybe...

"Yeah, sure, you're happy," he chuckled. She remained silent at the poor taste in laughter.

"You wouldn't use a gun either. The only gun you have access to is your boyfriend's, and you know his grief would be too unbearable once he realized one of his possessions ended your life. You'd use a razor. You would want the last minute high for nostalgia—and to numb the guilt," he continued, motioning his hands through the air. When he was alive, he often used his hands to speak.

Her eyes contorted with confusion. How could he possibly know? Her mouth filled with a million questions, but she couldn't force anything past her lips. Not even a breath. Her body froze but her mind was frantic. Was he really dead? Was he a ghost? Can dead people read minds? Nobody could have tipped him off because nobody knew. He seemed so certain about the razor, and was probably correct. Some of her best memories were when she was high with old friends, and to feel that way one more time would bring it all back. The feeling of weightlessness, like life slowly draining from her body; drifting into a dreamlike state, letting the guilt of her self-inflicted demise melt away in the pools of her own blood. How did he know that though? It had to be a crazy coincidence. Possibly a lucky guess.

She walked a few feet away from him toward the cliff that dropped 150 feet to the bottom of the canyon. For all he knows, she would just throw herself off the side of the cliff right now and be done with it. Ha! That would send him for a shock. Maybe he wasn't so smart after all.

"Too gruesome, and heights scare you," he said, beginning to toss his water bottle in the air. She spun around. That was no coincidence. He had just read her mind. It was an instant response to her immediate thought. She stared at his calm face, doing her best to hold onto her last thin string of composure.

"I can't read your mind," he said, replying to another one of her unspoken revelations.

"Says the guy who just answered my thoughts?" she retorted. With a sigh, he caught his water bottle mid-flip and began swinging it back and forth like a pendulum. His nonchalant attitude was both unnerving and oddly comforting. She stared at him, her eyes begging for answers.

"Okay, um, I'm not even sure where to start. So, you know how Sherlock Holmes makes educated assumptions based on visual clues?" he started. She squinted her eyes and nodded, knowing it had to be more than that. "It's kind of similar, I guess. Except I don't just use sight. I use every sense combined with what I learned about you after I died. I can pick up on the progression of your thoughts and make assumptions about how you will react to things because I know almost everything about you."

As much as her logical side resisted this explanation, part of her wanted to believe it was true. She didn't want him dead of course, but if he were dead, had he come back to help her? The idea would have filled her with a sense of relief if she didn't have so many questions weighing her down with stress. Could it be that he had ventured back from death to convince a long lost friend not to follow the same path?

"So, let's say it's true—you killed yourself," she purported as she kicked at bits of rock with the edge of her boot. "So here we are. Standing on this cliff in the middle of nowhere. And you knew I would accept your invitation to come out here because you now supposedly know everything. And you orchestrated this whole thing because you are going to tell me some magic remedy that will fix me and get rid of my depression. And you know I have depression. Which you know I have because you read my mind, which apparently you can do that now too. But you have no idea how it works," with a huff of frustration, she turned her back to him.

"I'm telling you, I'm not all-knowing. I can't read your

mind. I can just get a vibe about where your mind is headed." He reached out to touch her gently but pulled away thinking his touch would just upset her more. "And, I'm not going to take away your depression. I'm not going to take away your anxiety. I'm only here to save you," he told her attempting to disarm her obvious sarcasm.

"Oh, wow," she exclaimed, "you have got to be kidding me! It's one of those meetings, huh? About to whip out the ol' Bible and ask if I want to invite Jesus into my life?"

He started to laugh as he made the imaginary lock and key motion on his mouth again, reminding her that he couldn't discuss anything that happened after death. This gesture aggravated her to the core. Not many people have the chance to talk to a ghost. Out of all the ghosts she could speak to, of course, she was speaking to the one ghost that wasn't able to talk about being a ghost. She walked back to the boulder he had rested on just minutes before and leaned against it, trying to make sense of everything.

"Fine, so you're going to save me. Save me from what? So help me God if you say 'from yourself' I will grab my backpack and head out of here right now." She hated clichés. They might work in movies and books, but in the real world it usually meant that people hadn't put much effort into their response. He thought for a minute about his next words. She could see in his eyes that he had planned to say 'yourself' and now needed to backpedal. This gave her a brief feeling of control over the situation. She was now the one picking up on someone else's thoughts. Her chess pieces were back on the board, poised for a checkmate, and she suddenly felt very steady and confident. She was eager to see how he'd sidestep this one.

Instead of speaking, he walked to her backpack that still

lay in the dirt. He bent down and unzipped it, then stepped back leaving it where it sat. The look in his eyes demolished her short-lived smugness. Something was different now.

"What is it?" she asked him cautiously. He looked at her with deep concern, but still didn't speak. He lowered his head and lifted his palm gesturing toward the bag.

"So, you want to show me our water bottles and trail maps?" she joked, trying to hide her real feelings of apprehension.

She lifted herself from the boulder and walked toward the open bag. As she approached, he backed away. Bending to the ground, she opened the bag wider and peered inside of it. Yep, three water bottles and a mangled trail map. She looked back at him quizzically, but he stood completely still, hands shoved in his pockets and eyes fixated on the sky. He often did that when he was anxious, which heightened her own anxiety. Opening the mouth of the backpack wider and angling the sunlight into it, she saw a brief reflection in the bottom of the bag. Her heart started beating faster. Was it a ring—or a key? She reached in to retrieve the small object, pulled her hand out of the bag and uncurled her fingers to examine it. As soon as she laid eyes on it, her palm stiffened as she rose to her feet, trembling with fear. The image of a razor blade blurred as her tears began to cloud her vision.

"I... I didn't bring this," she could barely form the words. Her hand fell and the blade hit the ground with a small thump. Her breathing became erratic and tears now poured freely down her cheeks. She fell to her knees and hugged herself tightly, slowly rocking back and forth. She had packed the bag herself. How did that get in there? Why was it in there? How did he know about it? Then, the worst of all the questions fought its way to the forefront of her mind. Was she going to die today?

3

She knelt face-to-face with the menacing metal object. Momentarily entranced by its luster and shape as it stared back at her, she almost forgot where she was. Maybe she was just trying to forget. She had as many questions as she had tears falling down her cheeks. Besides her bewilderment about how the blade ended up in her bag and her fear about whether this signaled the end, another more gut-wrenching thought kept bursting through the dissonance in her brain. Did she deserve to die today?

That question seared her with guilt as if she had just struck a match in her head and the open flame was going to consume her from the inside out. She whispered these questions at the blade, as if it could answer back, and watched her tears pound the dirt below. The more she repeated the questions, the more her thoughts whirled while anxiety came over her in waves. It was enough to make her want to pick up the razor and slide it across her wrists to make it all stop. Her inability to control her thoughts was terrifying—how her thoughts could take command over her body so quickly and without mercy was terrifying. They had taken her to the end of the line more often than she could count. She had not only thought about suicide countless times, but had planned the details and even written a note. However strong her intentions were, she could never seem to commit to the next step. Seeing the razor in front of her, though, changed everything. She's the only one who could have put it in the bag. Had she intended on taking the final step today?

"You know you don't have to answer those questions,"

he said as a he pulled a string cheese snack out of his pocket. The sound of his voice lifted her head. She tried to spit out some words but her mouth was dry and unwilling as if she had just awoken from a deep sleep.

"Wha—what?" she managed. She felt dizzy, almost like a bad trip.

"Those questions you've been thinking about. The ones that are subconsciously urging you to do it. You think the only way to get rid of them is to answer them. I'm just saying, you don't have to." He sat on the ground and reclined backward, opening up the cheese and peeling a string off of it. She didn't really know how to react to his relaxed demeanor. So calm and collected when just a few moments ago he knew full well that the discovery of the razor blade almost destroyed her world and still might. His casual approach would have been almost offensive if she wasn't so curious about why he was acting this way. His response in general was confusing. She didn't have to answer them? What did he mean by that? Those questions are important, aren't they?

"How...how are you like that right now?" she eased out of her vocal chords, one small step at a time.

"Like what?" he asked, dangling the string of cheese above his mouth and nipping at it like a dog playing with a toy.

"You're so relaxed! In the midst of such a totally fucked up situation! You're dead. I didn't know you were dead. You don't seem dead. Then you're reading my most private thoughts. I don't remember putting that razor in my bag at all, and to top it off you're saying the questions I've been battling with for years don't matter?" she ranted.

He chewed on the cheese while pondering his answer,

then swallowed. Grinning, he sat up from the ground, "do you remember what you were doing when I called you to go to the canyon with me?"

She thought about it for a moment. She really didn't remember much. "I remember...I remember the phone ringing. I remember people talking. I felt rushed around. I'm confused...I can't...I'm having a hard time recalling much of anything except picking you up today and driving here." She shook her head as if trying to conjure up the memories. When they didn't come, she started breathing rapidly and her chest felt constricted. He slowly knelt down to her level and extended his hands to comfort her.

"Calm down, breathe. It's okay," he assured her.

She held her chest, struggling to fill her lungs with air. She didn't understand what was happening to her. "How can you say it's okay?" she summoned the strength to exclaim as she sprung to her feet. He stood up to meet her as she backed away from him. "I don't remember anything! What is happening? Why don't I remember anything? What did you do to me?" she cried out, pointing at him accusingly.

"I didn't do anything to you, I promise. I don't know why you don't remember," he said gesturing with his hands for her to calm down.

"You better start explaining yourself right now!" she screeched at him, slamming her foot down. She could no longer tolerate his evasive manner and was grasping for clues that she wasn't going insane.

"All I remember," he began, "is waking up this morning standing outside my parents' house with my phone. I immediately called you, invited you for a hike, and now we're here."

Her hand, shaking, lowered down to hold her stomach.

Her other hand clasped her forehead as she tried to regain composure. "You're a dead man! How can I trust anything you say to me?"

His efforts clearly weren't working. How could he win her trust so they could get back on track? Thinking quickly, he picked up a stick from the ground and walked over to where the dirt was softer. He stuck it into the ground and began to write something. "Look!" he yelled at her as he finished writing. She turned to face him. "Come read this."

Tentatively, she stepped over toward him. As she approached and saw his etchings in the dirt, the fire in her eyes faded into an expression of surprise and relief. She took a full breath and exhaled slowly. Those words on the ground changed her entire perception of why they were there and how much he knew about her.

"Alright, let's talk," she surrendered. As her agitated demeanor left her body, she slowly unfolded her arms and walked toward the razor. Sitting down next to it she held her head in her hands. He sighed with relief that he may have finally gotten her to engage. He dropped the stick to the ground, walked over to the razor and picked it up. He paced back and forth until he finally stopped and held the blade up to the sun that now fully lit the canyon. Examining it, he felt grateful he could convince her to stay and listen. Now for the hard part.

"Do you know why I used a gun?" he asked staring at the piece of metal in the hot sun. She lifted her head and set her lips against her hands, grateful the focus was off her for a moment.

"No, why did you?" She didn't know much about guns other than the constant political debates they incited.

"It's much faster. I couldn't stand the idea of falling from somewhere high. Oh, and the pain of a razor sliding across my skin?" He shuddered as he lowered the blade from the sky, standing to face her. "Unbearable. It's funny, I remember exactly how I felt about each way I could have killed myself, but I don't remember actually pulling the trigger once I chose my method. Just black. I remember thinking it was for the best. I remember the pain in my chest that was screaming for me to do it, and I remember all the hatred that coursed through my body. Then, like the calm before a storm, I felt numb. I didn't think about me, I didn't think about anyone else. The gun was against my head and everything went black."

They sat in silence as her mind digested his words. She had felt the same way before, just moments earlier. When she saw the razor, for a small chunk of time she didn't feel anything. She didn't think about anyone. It was just her and the razor co-existing in a common space.

"I don't want to die," she said, shifting her gaze to meet his.

"Not right now you don't," he said turning toward the cliff, gazing out over the sun drenched canyon. She followed him with her eyes.

"What do you mean by that?" She thought it was an awful thing to tell someone struggling with suicidal thoughts.

"Here comes a truth that will be very difficult to swallow," he said sighing. He turned away from the view he was enjoying and walked back to her. She watched him approach until they were sitting face-to-face. She studied his eyes. They weren't full of warm embraces now, but looked as hard and rugged as the boulders surrounding them.

He began, "most people prefer to avoid acknowledging

that life is never going to be 'happily ever after.' It's too difficult of a prospect to face. Even after we've come out on the other side of seemingly hopeless struggles, there will always be more to conquer. That reality is what leads us time and time again to a suicidal path."

At this, she felt her waves of anxiety returning and her chest became tight. Wasn't seeing the razor in plain daylight bad enough? Apparently, she had made up her mind and already chosen the tool of her demise. Wasn't this enough pain for one day? He was preaching no hope, no way out, and no relief from now until forever. Had he no mission other than to drag her down with life's ugly truths?

"You're *not* going to live happily ever after," he repeated for emphasis, as if hearing it once hadn't crushed her soul sufficiently. He tilted the razor back and forth in the sunlight, watching the reflections bounce off at different angles. "You're never going to be consistently okay. You'll have even lower moments than the ones today. You'll be kicked to the ground where no one can see you nor know the depths of your pain, except for this tiny razor blade. You will feel like your only escape will be sliding that blade across your wrist."

She had no capacity to endure any more of his "help." She longed for all the times they had been at that very spot in the past—him laughing, comforting her, caring for her. She was emotionally and physically spent, and his talk of future gloom seemed like unnecessary salt in her gaping wounds.

"So, I'm always going to feel this way...until I finally... do it?" she wearily whispered as she sank deeper into the pit of angst. "This is inevitable? There's no hope?" If there is no hope then there was no point going on. She could not muster the strength to referee the battleground of her mind forever.

He stopped fiddling with the razor blade and gazed at her. She sat in the dirt hunched over, her face stained with tears. He could feel her brokenness. He needed to make her understand. As she anticipated his answer, she saw his eyes were no longer hard like boulders, but soft and full of compassion. A light breeze blew between them and the red dirt of the canyon kicked up into the air, dancing with his monologues.

"Listen to me right now. There is always hope. Don't ever think that it is inevitable," he spoke sternly. Not out of anger but an urgency to force her to hear his words and make her understand their truth. She could see his attempts, but none of it was resonating with her. She was shutting down. Too much confusion. Too many contradictions. If there was hope, how was the worst yet to come? She couldn't live every day knowing that the next day could be worse. It wasn't worth it. Not worth the energy. Not worth the struggle.

"Yes, it is worth it," he replied to her thoughts.

"Oh, get fucked!" she exclaimed to herself. Worth it? Probably the most overused saying in the book, by her standards. Meaningless words. Who's to say what's worth it to her? Nobody knew the enormity of her pain. She was furious. He was an all-knowing ghost and the best answer he could give her was some bullshit cliché. Her anger gave her a sudden boost of energy as she pushed herself up from the ground. He followed suit.

"How the fuck do you know what's worth it for me?" she spat. "Who are you to say why I should want to live?"

"Why are you looking to others for a reason to be alive?" he demanded. He was not swayed by her anger. He had clearly anticipated this reaction, which added fuel to her rage.

She clinched up her hands into fists. He may claim to

know a lot about her, but she certainly didn't look to others for her reason to exist. She was independent enough—wasn't she?

"But you *are* looking to others, aren't you? I'm not anyone to say what makes life worth it for you. Neither is your boyfriend. Neither is your family. Do you stay alive for them? Are you nothing but a battery powering the shell of a body waiting until the one day you're worn out and die?" he continued.

Her anger boiled. He still remained calm and unaffected as she was losing her mind. They hadn't spoken in five years, and all of a sudden he knew her better than she knew herself? Still, a part of her was intrigued by his words, though her pride would never admit that. Was she only alive to keep others happy? When was the last time she thought about herself? What she needed? What she wanted? Thinking like that is selfish, right?

"Life is only worth it when you decide to make it worth it," he said putting his hands behind his back and pacing around the dirt. He picked up the stick again and twirled it absentmindedly as he walked circles around the words he had written earlier. She understood the words he spoke but didn't see the path to get there.

Her anger was beginning to diffuse as she tried to concentrate on any possible truth behind his assertions. The more she tried to understand, the more she felt the waging war of anguish and perseverance inside her head. One side was fury and hatred—the other was curiosity for the future and wanting to be better. She slowly walked back to her spot and sat down again. From the outside it appeared her fury had subsided, but he could see something much deeper than that inside her. The intensity of her internal conflict.

"How? How do I win this and get myself there?" she probed desperately. He could only look at her with concern and a bit of apprehension. He was not necessarily prepared to coach her through the specifics, but pressed on anyway.

"You can feel it, can't you?" he asked under his breath. "The battle inside your head. Right now. Part of you wants to shut me out and leave. The other part wants to hear me out. You're stuck in this conundrum, screaming for one side to win, then the other." He felt her desperation. Sympathetically, he rushed toward her and fell to his knees looking directly into her eyes. She was taken aback, and felt momentarily awkward by his close proximity. But, realizing his reaction was genuine, her defenses melted away.

"You don't have to pick a side." His eyes frantically searched hers for a hint of understanding, but her face remained blank. What did he mean? Of course one side has to win. What side could overtake the other? Which was she going to choose? What was she supposed to choose?

"Stop," he told her firmly, his eyes fixated in earnest. "You control the battlefield. You control every thought that goes through your head." His eyes wouldn't leave her no matter how many times she glanced away. He was adamant on getting his point across. "You are in control. Take ownership of both sides. Everything that happens in your mind is on you and you alone. Own your mind. The battle only wages because you're allowing it to go on. Shut it down and reconstruct what you want. Not what your emotions want. Listen to me or don't. Leave or stay. Whatever you do, make that decision based on what you want. On what logic says. Not your emotions. Not some fictional battle inside your head."

Own her mind. Shut the battle down. His words that echoed inside her head were strong and convincing. Figure out what she wants. Ignore both sides and look at the facts. She must make a decision. Just her; not her emotions. No one had ever put it to her like that.

A feeling of empowerment rose within her. Everyone gave advice on how deal with life better, how to handle emotions, how to manage conflict. No one had ever told her to take the wheel and drive quite like he just had. Still, how could she own her mind when people constantly tried to infiltrate it, take control, and hurt her?

His eyes still fixated on her, but were soft and reassuring. She climbed to her feet, but he remained on his knees gazing up at her.

"What about when someone hurts me and tries to take control? What then? When I get kicked down and I can't trust anyone?" She caught a glance of the razor that lay next to him, reminding herself that it would be the only thing keeping her company when life inevitably knocked her down. She stared at it with contempt. He smiled and pushed himself off the ground, standing up. He knew she had seen the razor, but chose to ignore that fact.

"Well, that's when you'll know what I mean by controlling your mind," he explained. She sighed, annoyed at his inability to, once again, explain himself clearly.

"You'll see—it's not about what other people do to you. It's about how well you can control your reaction. One truth is, people will always push you out of the way. People will always betray you, use you, and show you the worst in themselves. This simple fact also gives us a glimpse at another truth. If people will inevitably betray you, then your reaction to them is where you have control and can choose how to live your life. Our happiness can't be created by the actions of other people. It works both ways."

She went to interrupt him, ready to nail him on an inconsistency. Of course people can make other people happy. It's one of the things people were built for. To lift each other up.

"Let me finish," he said smiling. "Other people can make you feel happy, obviously. You're right about that. It's important and needed. The majority of people won't betray you or kick you down. All I'm saying is that happiness is not solely found in other people. The majority of happiness and true contentment is found when somebody pushes you down and you react out of kindness and love. Then you will realize that you have the power, not them."

It was starting to make sense to her. It seemed so simple. When someone riled up the whirlwind of dangerous thoughts in her head, she could decide to lasso and subdue it. But if it was this straightforward, how had it eluded her all these years? The frustrating part of mental battles was that the solution always sounded great in theory, but the execution was the tricky part. It was one of the reasons she hated clichés so much—that flowery, optimistic fluff perpetuated by movies and books often fell flat in the real world. Things never seemed to work out when she longed for the sun to shine on her face again.

4

Engulfed by darkness, my face boiled with heat. Unaware that I was slowly losing breath my chest pounded heavily, gasping as my eyes darted back and forth. I was completely oblivious to the darkness that surrounded me. Underneath my eyelids, I dreamt only of loss and heartache; never knowing where my dream ended and my reality started. Dark and clouded with sudden bursts of a nightmare fantasy that would ultimately lead me to where I would end up that morning. Pressure pushed against my head. An odd combination of softness and heaviness that began to slowly suffocate me. The only thing to relieve this torture was a faint jingle I heard every twenty-four hours for all of my life.

I slowly opened my eyes and the cloud of death dissolved as I stared at the square of light illuminating the small space above it. My phone droned on and on, demanding my attention. I moved my right arm off the pillow that was crushing my head, and the pressure dissipated. The darkness subsided and the morning light spilled onto my face. My body, soaked with sweat, was cruelly reminded that my air AC was broken.

I lay gazing at the phone that wouldn't stop until it had received some sort of proof that I was awake. I didn't move. The chorus went on and on. I knew if I turned it off, I would be forced to get up and see that no one was lying next to me. Alone again. So instead I lay staring at it. The ultimatum I had made the night before—if I felt any different today—was looking more like a losing bet as I thought about the trip I would likely be making to the canyon. I had convinced myself that if it felt different, I would trudge on and follow the path where I had always found myself. If I didn't, I would skip a few steps to the welcoming handshake of death at the canyon.

I thought about it often and found a weird sense of comfort doing so. The way out. The one thing I could do to escape the monotony I of my life. The one thing that would free me from ever putting on this shitty mask I wore every single day. I sat up in bed and there it was. The heartache, the beautiful disaster that is my life. Beautiful only in the sense that life is inherently beautiful, but disastrous in the way that my life would be taken from me.

I didn't think about her often, so I wasn't just a lonely guy pining for a girl. Maybe I was, though. It's true I didn't think about her often, but that day I did. I ran my hands over the spot where she used to lay her head. My emptiness was palpable. I hadn't spoken to her in years and knew nothing about her life. She could have been married for all I knew. I'd like to believe that I would have been happy for her, but I don't think I had that capacity. The first sign of not truly loving her, I suppose.

I sat up and grabbed my phone off the nightstand. As usual, no messages. I was cruelly reminded of all the times she would wake up to a thousand messages from other guys. I never felt jealous, because she was next to me, not them. I walked to my bathroom, flipped on the light, and lifted the lever to start the shower. Mindlessly, I stared at the water flow that was bound to wake me up before my journey. As the warm water dripped down my body I tried not to think much. A theme that would carry on throughout the day. I was always an overthinker, but for whatever reason that day, my mind was silent. The quiet before the storm perhaps.

I stared at the soap sitting in the shower's corner. No need for that today, I surmised. In fact, the only reason I was even in the shower was to bring me to full consciousness. I wondered about who would come to my funeral. Who cared enough about me to say goodbye? Lots of people, I imagined. A common misconception about people who are suicidal. At least, it was for me. Most people believe that those planning to kill themselves think nobody will care. On the contrary, I fully believed my funeral would be filled with people who loved and cherished me. So why do it, then? Why take something away from them? I was only living for them, and could not be my own man. I was sinking in this quicksand of people I only existed for, and it consumed my being. I was emotionally and socially drained to the point of no return. My battery had died.

No, that's not why I was doing it. For me, it wasn't one big reason. At my funeral, I was sure there would be fifty different people giving fifty different reasons for why I did it, and each one would be absolutely right. It was like a spiderweb of thoughts and emotions in my head. Each line just as important as the next for this web to be spun.

I turned the shower off and dried myself. I threw on some clothes and grabbed my backpack, loaded with a few water bottles. Then, I added something else. Something that would change the tone of the entire day.

I put the gun into my backpack next to the water bottles. I looked down at it while it stared back at me. That inanimate object would potentially take a life today. Life, if it was even worthy to be called that. From here on out, everything felt like a very cinematic movie. Not that I was an actor playing a character of myself, or even a character that inevitably would find himself at a crossroads. No, it was the moments in a movie when you're just enjoying the cinematography. Long, lingering shots of the gun and me staring at each other. A wide shot of me zipping up my backpack with the sun bleeding through the blinds and creating the slightest amount of lens flare. The light breaking through the darkness as if there may be some sign of hope, but the audience would have to keep watching to see.

Music begins to play in the background, maybe something obscure and instrumental or maybe something popular to convey the emotion the audience should be feeling. I thought about this as I stared at the gun. At least the audience would know how to feel even if I didn't. I closed my bag and turned around to pick up an envelope that sat on my coffee table. It was addressed to "Everyone." A letter I had written the night before. A letter that would explain everything. Full of anger and hatred. Full of random thoughts and probably from the opinion of the outside world, insanity. I opened the envelope to give it one last read:

Dear Everyone,

I guess I should tell everyone how sorry I am but the truth is that I'm not and I'm not around anymore to care about what you think anyways, or maybe I am. Who knows really. I guess I'll find out. To my parents, yup, you were parents. You did everything you could to make me happy. You gave me a roof over my head, gave me a car, paid for my school, only ever tried to make me happy. I'm writing this letter because I am anything but happy. Because of you guys? No, well, I don't know. Some of it has to do with you. I should be happy but I'm not. The world is at my fingertips and everything just slips away with time. It's not really the individual strokes I'm unhappy with, it's the overall painting. What I mean by that is that I hate my life but individual things I don't. I overthink everything and when people find out then I end up overthinking even more. I start to like and care for someone and then get too attached and then they tell everyone they know that I get too attached and so then everyone else thinks I'm that way and all their friends think I'm a bad person for it so I can't even make friends because I'm the annoying attached guy that can't get over people or be alone. Side note, if you tell someone they need to learn to be alone then get fucked. From the beginning of time, humanity was designed to be with other people or even one person. Humans are not designed to be alone. What? Are you going to tell me that the bum that dies and had no one at his funeral should have just learned to be alone? And why don't you tell that to people that are in relationships? Go ahead. Go tell that friend that's been dating that girl for two years that he needs to break up with her so he can "learn to be alone." Get fucked. That's the bullshit sentiment so you don't have to actually think for a goddamned minute about what might actually be the problem and that no one is meant to be alone. Where was I, oh yeah, I'm the annoying guy that everyone "likes" but nobody wants to actually talk to or hang out with. "Hey man, good to see you let's hang out sometime!" Then I put myself out there to do something and it's always they're busy or they cancel or they never answer because they already have friends. There are plenty of people that are going to know I'm dead. I don't doubt that at all. I don't doubt that it'll hurt some people. Maybe people will actually think though. That would be nice. Think about actually hanging out with someone every once and a while or call someone or texting them. Stop treating people like we're just things that take up space. Moving on, I might come back to it but who knows. She's still on my fucking mind. It's been years since we've even spoken. We split ways and it was supposed to be a clean break. I don't know anything about you anymore and that breaks my heart still. I don't blame you if you hate me. I fucking hate my life. I hate getting up in the morning. I hate sitting on my couch and not doing anything. "Go out and do stuff!" cool you want to fucking hang out? No? Didn't think so you fucking asshole. God I hate that shit. "Go meet people!" Oh yeah? Just like that? God fuck off. You don't get it because you already have friends that you can meet other people through. I don't know anybody. I'm not a good person. I don't know if god exists. I don't know if heaven or hell exists. That's the only thing that's kept me for so long from pulling the trigger. That there's a chance I could end up burning in eternal fire or being tortured for eternity. Yeah, that's a real fear of mine. And it's the only thing keeping me breathing. I guess I just got to the point where I rationalized burning forever or being tortured forever. I love people. I really do. But people don't love me and don't want anything to do with me. Don't say that's not true. Don't. If it were true then I would have friends. I would have people who text me that they want to hang out instead of me always having to put in the effort. Always. Look through my phone, go ahead. Everyone I text, I TEXT. No one ever texts me first. I'm that fucking guy. Learn to be alone! Says everyone that has friends, family, and are in a relationship. No one ever did this while I was alive. Try to put yourself in my shoes. Turn off your phone and social media for a month. Go to work. Go home. Watch tv and eat. And repeat for a month. That's my life. Every day. Oh except I desperately try to get people to hang out or people to just talk to me and I get nothing. So it's a daily process of disappointment. Why do you think I have a tinder? I get a little joy any time someone says hi to me. Because no one likes me. So then there must be something wrong with me. I'm annoying. I'm ugly. I'm too sexual. I'm too loud. I'm dirty. I'm too this, I'm too that. Don't make a list of bad things! Be confident! I can't fucking be confident when literally everything about me as a person pushed people away. I wonder what they'll say. It doesn't matter now. I just looked up a bunch of different suicide letters. Am I doing this wrong? I'm supposed to be saying how sorry I am and how bad I feel? I don't really feel sorry. I feel a lot of anger and betrayal and numbness. I feel actually mostly numb. I keep staring into nothing just trying to justify this. Nothing really ever justifies it because that means I have to justify it from your perspective. And without you knowing that I'm writing this or planning this then all you can say is "Cheer up buddy! Go meet people! Learn to be alone!" Nothing will ever justify this because you will always find a reason to find it unjustifiable. I'm leaving now and I'm not coming back.

I wasn't happy with what I had written. I didn't care about the grammar. I was going to die that day, my mind was made up. I wasn't going to waste my time with figuring out the perfect words to say when my journey was about me and not what they were going to think of me. Why would they care anyway? I tossed the letter on the coffee table, grabbed my keys and threw my backpack over my shoulder, feeling the weight of the gun on my back. I had never felt anything so heavy. I opened the door and slammed it shut. Walking outside, I stopped at the sound of a loud crash that came from inside. Opening the front door again, I looked inside and saw that my blinds had fallen to the floor. Light flooded the living room. For a moment, I thought about fixing them, but decided someone else should do that. I closed the door and, for the last time, locked it. The black of night had been erased by the emerging blue sky of morning. The cool air brushed against my skin, my hoodie protecting me from the chill. A few hours from now, the heat would burn up the canyon air, my lifeless body along with it.

5

He pulled his water from her bag and swirled the half full bottle, watching a small cyclone form inside. Every so often he would stop the motion of his wrist and watch until the water stilled. Then, he would start it in the opposite direction until the cyclone reappeared.

"Why did you do it?" she asked, as he focused on the water spinning round and round. She had a nagging need to settle the uncertainty in her head. He sat in silence not answering. For a moment, she thought he was just contemplating his answer, but as more time passed she realized he was ignoring the question. Stepping closer to him as he leaned against a boulder still swirling his bottle, she wondered if she shouldn't have asked. Was this too hurtful a subject to broach? Killing himself couldn't be easy to reflect upon. Then again, he was the one who had brought it up in the first place. She needed to know, but still felt hesitant to verbalize it.

"Was it because of me?" she blurted out suddenly. She clasped her hands to her mouth; surprised the words had come out. How selfish of her to think someone was that obsessed with her. That he would take his own life because she refused to be with him. She wished she could grab the words out of the air and stuff them back in. She slowly lowered her hand and sat in awkward silence. She could see in his eyes that he was intending to answer, but was choosing his response carefully.

"Why do *you* want to do it?" he broke the silence by turning the tables on her, still staring at his swirling water. She swung her foot and stepped in slow motion as she pondered why. She glanced around at the ground, the trees, and the canyon ledges. A twirl of dead leaves flowed by her feet carried by a soft breeze. She watched them dance around the air, wondering what it was that had killed them. It was springtime so they should be blooming with life; just as she should.

She was having difficulty defining her reason. Why *did* she want to do it? She didn't have a terrible life. She had many people who loved her and were happy when she was around. She had a good paying job and never had to worry about bills. She laughed often. To an outsider, her life probably appeared lovely and fulfilling.

"I'll ask again, why do it?" he questioned almost flippantly, his water still spinning. She stopped pacing long enough to stare at him and the bottle he was so fascinated with. She waited for eye contact, but there was none. He seemed strangely disconnected to this serious question he posed. Could he not see why she was struggling to answer? Since nobody knew her secret, this was the first time she had ever been asked this question.

She longed for more compassion as she sorted out her feelings, but it seemed like the water in his bottle was the only thing he cared about. She felt confused and somewhat invisible. Maybe this was the lesson. Maybe she was so focused on him and his reactions that she couldn't adequately concentrate and reflect on her own critical answer. She never had to justify her reason, so she never really pinpointed one.

He continued to stare into his water. She felt the only way to get a reaction from him was to just get it out. With a short pause and quick breaths, she began to verbalize these feelings for the first time.

"When I wake up in the morning, I don't feel awake or tired. All I feel is a burning weight on my chest that's crushing my ribs until they're stabbing into my heart. I roll over and see my boyfriend getting ready for work and think, 'Why am I not happy? Is it him? It can't be. He's perfect.' I go to work and put on a mask for everyone because if they saw the actual face underneath, no one would understand. I know that my past is behind me, but I still can't get over the dark thoughts that creep into my head. Every day I go through this routine of being an adult and I can't break free. Every day I take care of my responsibilities and walk a little bit further down this path and closer to the inevitable hand of death at the end. The path is daunting. I want so badly to bypass all the bullshit in between and just skip to the end. Even if I had everything I ever wanted in life, it still puts me on this path of going to school, getting married, getting a secure job, paying bills, retiring, and then death. This is the cycle that everyone from janitors to doctors face, and it's the cycle that nobody talks about. But, it's the cycle I can't stop thinking about and it's weighing so heavily on my chest every single morning that I can't breathe. And I can't tell anyone because they would say that stupid cliché about life being a roller coaster and we all need to learn to just enjoy the ride and—FOR GOD'S SAKE WILL YOU STOP STARING AT YOUR FUCKING BOTTLE AND LISTEN TO ME?!"

Her chest now lifted and lowered as she took deep, agitated breaths while he continued to fixate on his water with childlike fascination. He had gone through the trouble of bringing her to the canyon and professing he was there to save her, but now sat silent when she needed help sorting out her tangled thoughts. Her intensity was escalating as she had begun to both discover and articulate why she thought about suicide so often and why she wanted to do it. She was stuck on the same path that she saw everyone else following, and she hated it. Hatred for the path had morphed into hatred for her life. In her eyes, there was no escape from this path. She wasn't sure she could continue to trudge on. She hoped he had some insight for her. Some wisdom.

He finally stopped swirling the bottle and gathered his thoughts as the water settled. She waited in anticipation for his words. "I guess some of it was because of you," he replied, answering her question from minutes before, without even acknowledging her revelation about the dreaded cycle and her despised path. In disbelief, she waited for him to continue, but he said nothing more. Just as he had mentally checked out by swirling his water, she decided it was her turn to appear unengaged. Two could play this game. She rolled a small rock around with her foot, pretending to not care or need his counsel. Not getting any reaction from him, especially after divulging her most personal thoughts, was another wound to add to her collection of jabs that day.

Watching her now, and possibly seeing through her motives, he finally added, "How could it not be somewhat because of you? Just looking at this water—it goes around and around until I steady my hand and it quiets. Problems in my life would swirl around and around and sometimes they would subside. Like when I thought I was getting over you. Then, when everything seemed settled, I stirred the waters again with negative thoughts and emotions until there was no stopping the storm I'd created."

Was it really just that? She pondered the simplicity of his explanation. Just an array of problems ebbing and flowing over time until he felt the force of his hand pulling the trigger?

"It was more than that," he continued. "All I'm saying is that problems come and go constantly. Water cyclones into a storm and a few moments later steadies into the quiet whole-someness of the life we all love." He finally set down his water bottle next to the boulder and stretched his arms out.

"It was the cycle for me also. I guess that's part of the reason I'm the one meeting with you. I saw ups and downs in my future. Responsibilities, mortgage payments, 401(k), promotions, more work. Day after day after day. I didn't see a way out and I didn't want that life—as a doctor, nor as a janitor. Add in a little spice of all the other problems swirling around, plus being alone most days, and I found myself with a pretty big ego."

Ego? What did he mean by ego? That's not at all what she expected. It sounded like the perfect storm for depression or anxiety. The last thing she expected was for him to say ego. If anything, it sounded like his ego would've been crushed by self-hatred. She didn't understand.

"It's ego. Trust me. People never want to face it because it means they probably have to tear it down. That's what's terrifying about your own ego. It can grow so large that it looks like a natural part of you, even making you feel self-righteous and incredibly humble. Just like cancer replacing every healthy part of yourself until it devours you completely, ego takes over your entire character and humanity. It's extraordinarily tricky to master in your own head. I blamed everything in my life on other people because I, of course, couldn't be at fault. It was my dad's fault for getting angry at me, my mom's fault for forgetting to tell me something, my coworker's fault for messing up an order at work, your fault for destroying our relationship. Everything was everyone else's fault and, what was worse, is that I blamed them for the way I acted. I blamed my anger, depression and anxiety on everyone else because, in my head, they were the ones who caused it. I could never be the one at fault. My ego was so big that I couldn't even take responsibility for my own emotions.

Then, when you add in the decent money I made, my investments, the house I owned—everything—it was simple to justify my ego. Everything was in order. Everything was perfect for my ego to thrive. It felt like a well-oiled machine churning inside my head. Everyone else made me feel terrible about myself, but I told myself I wasn't a bad person. How could someone who had everything be a bad person?"

It made sense to her when she thought about ego in the context of *his* life. Too bad it didn't help her at all. She was nothing like that. Her ego wasn't big at all. Everything about her was meant for others. She was exhausted by the constant barrage of people leaning on her. It was never her leaning on them.

"But, something was still wrong," he added. "I had the excuses. I had the ego. I had the money, the house, the everything. In my mind, I had it all checked off my list. So why didn't I feel like I had everything under control? Why did I still wake up with a weight on my chest? Why did I feel like I was only one bad day away from ending it all? I had this perfect machine but something was still missing. And, unfortunately, I never figured it out until I ended it all."

She was so drawn to his explanation that without realizing it, she had stopped pretending to ignore him. She was soaking up his words and was waiting for him to reveal the key element that possibly could have kept him alive. He cleared his throat as he prepared to divulge it.

"Purpose. A goal. My machine was redlining but had nowhere to go. Ego made sure of that." His face went stone cold.

"What? Are you serious right now? I would've almost preferred for you to say that religion was your missing piece." She had goals. She had dreams. How was this supposed to help her? He stood up straight.

"Do you? Do you have goals? Do you know the steps you're taking every day to reach those goals? You think you don't have a big ego, but the first thing you did when I told you I killed myself was to assume it was some way to get you back. Your ego is just as big as mine was, if not bigger. Just like me, you're failing to own it and you're no closer to your goals than you were five years ago," he scolded.

She couldn't stand that he was getting heated with her. She wasn't some child that needed to be taught discipline. She was an adult that struggled with a very serious condition, and disparaging a person in her state wasn't right. He was causing her anxiety to crescendo. How dare he talk to—

She swiftly put the brakes on her train of thought and clasped her hand across her chest at her sudden revelation. He knew she had seen a glimpse of her ego for the first time, and he raised his eyebrows and nodded at her in confirmation. It was her ego making her offended at his line of accusations. She thought about all the things she had done in her life that were basically a product of this shadowy figure that loomed over her. This thing called ego was much larger than she had ever realized. It had been there the whole time, sucking life out of her and forcing her to be something she didn't even know she was.

"Your ego is one of the biggest things keeping you from living your life," he explained, "and the main thing that keeps you thinking about the endless cycle."

"Why does it work so well for other people, then? Some people are so happy on their paths, but I constantly feel like I can't break free?" She posed these questions with intent and purpose. After discovering these new truths about herself she couldn't wait to learn how to get out.

"We're all made differently. Some people can handle

where they are just fine. Others, like you and me, have a mixed bag of chemicals in our brains that don't want to cooperate with the normal world. It doesn't make you any less, and it doesn't make them any less." She thought it was interesting how he said it doesn't make them any less, and didn't phrase it as any more.

"Why would I say any more? The others aren't more. The idea of what I'm saying is that you are on equal ground with people who can handle the cycle of life. But following a path that was not built for you will inevitably lead you to misery."

"Why do you say chemicals in my brain?" She had heard this before but mostly thought it was bullshit. She saw plenty of other people digging themselves out of sad situations and choosing to be happy, so why couldn't she?

"Don't ever put that on yourself. Like I said, some people can operate under the normalcy of life and they thrive. Others, like you, need help to align the chemicals in their heads. Some people can simply choose to be happy and it works, but for you it's a harder fight. It's not a simple choice and it never will be." She rolled her eyes. She remembered where she had heard something similar, and it was from the therapist she had seen for a long time.

"Yeah, so you want me back on medication. Is that it?" she asked.

"This isn't a joke," his tone of voice drew her eyes to his. "This is a literal fight every day for your very life. You think medication won't help because of some egotistical notion that it'll make you less of a person or that you can handle things yourself. Take ownership of that ego and listen to me. You need every bit of help you can get in this battle, and medication is a sword to fight with. You will lose every time if you go in unarmed."

She looked away, irritated. "Then why do other people, even some of them with depression, not have to take meds? Huh? I'm not strong enough, but they are?"

"It's not about whether you're strong enough—it's about living!" he yelled in her face. She went quiet. He lowered his stance, breathing heavily. "Winning this fight is the top priority. If you won't use every tool to win this fight then it's already over."

She hadn't taken medication in almost a year. She didn't like the way it made her feel, and she didn't care for her therapist either.

"Then you find another one," he immediately responded to her thought.

"What?" she asked turning around to face him.

He raised his eyes to meet hers. "You find another one. You can have a fighting chance, but finding the right help is key. One therapist didn't work. Go to another one. You can and will find the help you need. But before you do any of that, you have got to own and control your ego that's almost completely replaced you."

She didn't like the idea of finding another therapist. How could she find a good one? What if she didn't like the new one? The thought of it mentally exhausted her, but, she also knew that she thought more and more about suicide and the fight did seem harder with each passing day. She had been feeling so alone and without any hope, despite all of the people in her life who loved her.

"There's a way out of this cycle—a way off this path. You'll have to change your behavior first, though. Starting with your ego. The alternate path requires you to be tough, smart, and most of all, humble."

All of her false bravado crumbled and there were no more games. "Show me. Please. I don't want to die. I want to know how to manage this. Please," she whispered under her breath.

"I am showing you. You're seeing behind the curtain now. You're getting it. You're realizing that it's not something that will go away, but there is hope with the right help. You're getting that there is more than just one path. There's a way out of the cycle. You're learning that you have to take charge of your ego. It all starts right there. You're stuck on that path because you choose to be. What time do you get up every day?"

At that question, his eyes that had just given her hope rapidly dragged her back down into lifelessness. Everyone says to get up early. She already knows she's supposed to get up early. She does get up early—at seven in the morning to go to work— every weekday, for years.

"I asked you what time you get up in the morning. I never said anything about how early." She rolled her eyes. This mind-dreading stuff, or whatever he called it, was exasperating.

"Yeah, but you know you were about to—"

"You get up because you have to go to work, right?"

"Uh...yes. I have to get up at seven," she reluctantly replied, gritting her teeth.

"You're kind of ruining the entire purpose of getting up early." He smiled at her. She was thoroughly annoyed and he knew it. He had pushed a button and was about to push many more until something broke.

"Please! Tell me what you mean!" She fake smiled and replied with an obvious air of sarcasm. He grinned and chuckled.

"Getting up early is supposed to be done for yourself. Not for work. It builds discipline. Feel free to jump in headfirst and do that. I care about your consistency."

She was consistent, though. She woke up at seven every day, minus the weekends when she was off work.

"Wake up at seven on the weekend, too. Keep it consistent."

"What? Why?" she asked, genuinely confused.

"You want off this path? So build your own path. Own it. Get up at six, even. You choose your daily routine. Not your boss, not your boyfriend, not your parents. You do."

This fraction of advice resonated with her. It wasn't about the actual waking up and getting ready for the day. It was about creating her own path that she wanted to be on.

"Exactly. It's clicking now," he said. He was right; it was making a connection with her. She started to smile a little. He looked at her and saw she seemed a bit more human than before. "Do you remember when we first met?"

Her eyes brightened. That was something she hadn't thought of in a very long time and wasn't something she expected to be discussing. She did remember, though. He was a suggested friend on Facebook and she had added him on a whim. They started a dialogue on Messenger and she invited him to a party she was throwing.

"I wouldn't exactly call four people sitting on your parents' couch watching Jim Carrey's version of "A Series of Unfortunate Events" a party," he laughed, scratching the back of his head.

"Hey, that movie is a cinematic masterpiece," she joked. She knew very well that the mediocre movie and the friends she invited over were a subtle ploy to meet him in person.

"I knew it! I knew that wasn't a real party!" he shouted with mock anger. She smiled and felt a bit embarrassed that she had been found out, even after all these years.

"Stop reading my mind! That was a great party that created lots of wholesome memories with my friends...," she paused trying to think of her friends' names. He pointed at her, smiling.

"Ha! You don't even remember your friends' names from that so-called party!" She only needed to remember one name. She only needed to remember one person from that night, him. They transformed from strangers to best friends in a short amount of time. After that party, they quickly progressed from acquaintances to soul mates, and then, as the Bible says, they became one flesh. In spirit, they were bonded like a strong married couple. In actuality, at least in her mind, they were best friends with some physical benefits on the side.

Their smiles and laughter quickly turned to silent sadness as they both remembered their ending. He wanted to be official and wanted her forever. She wanted to revert back to being just friends—without the intimacy. This was when the storms of fights broke out. Yelling and screaming almost every time they were together. He continued to put forth romantic gestures while she pursued new guys who swept her off her feet. The strain of their different wants and needs left them with no other option but to part ways. He was known for telling people they had broken up, though from her perspective, they had never actually dated. She was known for telling people that he couldn't handle just being friends.

"It doesn't matter now," he said flatly as he walked past her to where the blood stain lay across the ground.

6

"I'm not single now, anyway," she said under her breath with her back facing him. She heard a small chuckle escape from his mouth. He had thought the world of her when he was alive, which certainly didn't help her ego issue. For the past five years, she knew she always held a special place in his heart, as he did in hers. So why did he laugh at the idea of her having a boyfriend?

"I don't know why you're laughing," she responded, turning to look at him. "It's the most serious I've ever been with anyone." She felt as though she was being accused of not having a legitimate relationship and needed to defend it. Before today, she wouldn't have cared about getting validation from him, but somehow since he was dead and "all-knowing," she felt she needed it now. Almost like his opinion of her mattered more now that he was no longer in her world.

He covered his mouth to keep the small chuckle from escalating even louder. Her initial offense at his laughter quickly transformed into a wave of relief when she reminded herself that she didn't have to answer to him anymore. She remembered the jealous rages she constantly had to deal with, and was glad he no longer could try to lay claim over her. She didn't want this situation or discussion to be about the two of them.

"It's not. It's absolutely not about our relationship, or lack thereof. It's not about you and me, nor you and your boyfriend."

"Then why laugh?" she interjected.

"It's just that after all that about egos and medication and everything, you still think I would have brought you here today just to try to get back together with you?"

He was right again. No matter how much he already told her, her mind was constantly wandering back trying to decipher the real reason all this was happening. It was like she was in and out of a dream. Bits of it made sense, and then didn't. She would have a revelation, only for her thoughts to be clouded again. And, yes, a small part of her still questioned whether it was some sort of trickery—a dramatic and emotional scene he planned so he could be her knight in shining armor. Her still-intact ego somehow hoped it was, so she could have the satisfaction of still having the upper hand. The difference today; however, was that she now recognized this shadowy figure, and actually smiled at the realization.

It was nice to know that she could still smile through this fight. This fight for her...sanity? They had discussed the fight and ways to prepare herself. What exactly was she fighting for? To survive?

"Your fight to thrive as an individual. Your fight to live without the need of your boyfriend, family or friends."

Her heart sank. She was confused again and walked to her backpack, plopping herself down next to it so she could collect her thoughts. He had just spoken about using every tool to win the fight, but now he was talking about not relying on anybody to help win the fight. How could it be both? She relied heavily on her family, friends and boyfriend. She needed them and fully believed that she couldn't live without them.

"That's where you're wrong."

"But it's good to have friends. It's good to have support. You said it yourself—people can support you," she argued. She held her head in her hands. By this point, she thought she would've had a throbbing headache. The beating sun, the dry air, and the intense conversation were not only a perfect storm of depression and anxiety, but also the recipe for a killer headache. Nothing came, though. She stared at the dirt below her feet. Was he the reason for her lack of headache? She lifted her head and looked at him. This time he didn't give any indication at all that he knew what she was thinking.

"Of course it's good. People can push you forward when you feel like giving up, but it's not good to rely on them so heavily. They are not your batteries, just like you are not theirs. They are your support—not your lifeblood."

Still confused by the fact that she felt good physically, despite all that her mind and body had been through, she just rolled with the conversation to see where it would lead. She crossed her arms and turned away as he calmly picked up a stick and used it to push a pebble on the ground.

"Besides, it would be a waste to rely on someone so heavily like that. For either of you." She turned back to look at him. All her life she was taught by her teachers, parents, and friends that she needed them and they needed her. Humans were social beings. It was something to be celebrated, not torn down.

"What's that supposed to mean?" she inquired. She wasn't annoyed, but genuinely curious about what he meant. He stood quietly, continuing to push pebbles along the ground.

"Helping others is always right. Not replacing others' weaknesses with your own strengths, though—that hinders people from learning to grow to their full potential. Don't be their crutch, but help them learn to be strong. Then, in time, that person can use his or her strength to help others. Our intent should not be to push people out of the way and take credit for that person's growth or success while masking it as 'help.' We are meant to push each other forward so we can watch people achieve greater things than they ever could without our push." He pondered the words he just spoke while he allowed time for them sink into her mind. She actually did agree with him. People push each other forward, but when they rely too heavily on others, they eventually feel like they're not strong enough to do anything on their own.

"So, you're saying the reason I think about suicide is because I rely so heavily on other people that I, personally, see no reason to live?"

He stopped pushing the pebbles along the ground and smiled, still looking down.

"You're getting it. Ego, this, the storm turning the water into a cyclone. It has many strikes of lightning."

She sighed. She wanted this to be over now. She didn't hate being with him, nor learning how to help herself, but she was mentally exhausted. She lay on her back and closed her eyes. He walked over and sat down next to her.

"I know you're tired. The idea of taking your own life is a major wall that's been constructed inside yourself. It's going to take a lot of push and pain to tear it down."

She opened her eyes and stared deep into the blue sky with the few fluffy clouds overhead. She often liked to study the clouds and look for familiar shapes in them, but not now. She had no energy for imagination, puzzles or analogies. At this moment, all she wanted was for everything to be straightforward and real. As real as the wall inside her.

He was right. Tearing down that wall would be difficult. She longed to just pretend it wasn't there. That would be so much easier. She wanted her friends and family to distract her from thinking about that wall. She wanted to curl up into a ball and simply ignore it until...

"...until the thoughts of suicide build up so high that the wall falls in and crushes you and everyone around you. I know your wants. I know those thoughts feel like legitimate wants."

She turned over with her back facing him, sending a clear message that she didn't want to go down that road. But he knew that by acknowledging these feelings of discomfort she would be the first step in healing.

"I know that no matter how many times people tell you that you are loved, nothing ever feels like it can stop the looming presence of the wall you've built."

She noticed a slight change in his voice and sat up with her back still facing him. She had never heard this sound in his voice before. The only way she could describe it was a sharp cry with sudden pauses between words to breathe heavily. Yet, his voice was deep and moving. He was passionate about what he was saying and fully believed it. Not as if he wasn't being truthful before, but this truth carried extreme weight and conviction.

He sat in front of her and looked into her eyes. She looked away without even being conscious of it. She felt awkward because everything he said was true and she couldn't have felt more ashamed. She had so many people in her life who loved her. She was grieved that she would be selfish enough to take that away from them, but in the midst of depression, it was hard to think clearly and logically about such things. This made her hate herself even more and her wall grew larger and stronger instead of being deconstructed.

"Look at me," he pleaded. Still, she stared at the ground beside them. Tears stung her eyes as she thought about her friends to whom she had grown so close, and who all loved her so much. She thought about her aunt who had practically raised her after her childhood tragedy. She couldn't stand thinking of that poor woman going through yet another tragic loss in her family.

"Look at me," he repeated. The earnestness in his voice had lightened up, and now sounded gentle and welcoming. Her eyes slowly lifted and locked with his. He grinned at her and his eyes gave her the feeling of a warm embrace, just like they once had. It was like the hug a young boy gives his dad after he gets home from a hard day at work. The only thing the dad needs to get him through to the next day. The only thing she needed in this moment.

"I see you," he said slowly. She didn't know why she grinned at that. It was like when her aunt would try to embarrass her by singing in the middle of the grocery store. She would try to act angry, but couldn't hold in the smile for long. But, why would he say that? Just a few seconds ago he was in a stark, serious mood. He then does this? He sees her? What does that mean? It was ridiculous. She looked away again, her grin disappearing as she reminded herself of the gravity of the situation. This had been a traumatic and emotional day for her and she needed to know he understood that.

"No, look me in the eyes," he told her again. He now had a demanding tone. Normally she would ignore any guy who spoke to her in that manner, and would probably have walked away, but the uniqueness of this situation kept her engaged.

"I'm not just going to do whatever you say. I'm my own person. Forgive me if I'm a bit uncomfortable," she said sarcastically. "I can stare at the ground if I want to. This is serious and you're not acting like it. Your demeanor is all over the place, and it is making my emotional roller coaster even worse."

"Look at me," he demanded again, sounding even more intent on getting what he wanted. She could tell this power struggle was going nowhere. She could either throw a fit and walk away, or do as he asked and see where this rabbit hole lead. She lifted her eyes hesitantly toward his.

"I see you." This time he grinned. She couldn't hold hers in either, even letting go of a hint of a laugh but trying to hide it with a question.

"What are you doing? This is so stupid. Two seconds ago, you were serious and demanding. I just can't keep up with all these mood changes!"

He chuckled and continued to look deep into her eyes. Windows to the soul, she had heard them called. What was he looking at? Her small burst of laughter started to breathe life into her, and she began to laugh even harder.

"I see you," he repeated once again with a giggle.

"What? What do you see? Why are you doing this?"

They both laughed on top of the cliff where a man had committed a brutal evil. They felt incredibly silly as they watched each other's eyes and completely forgot about the atmosphere of dread and despair the cliff gave off. After a moment of laughter at each other, he stood up and wiped the tears of joy from his eyes.

"The wall is only there if you let it be," he told her. "Even something as simple as just looking into your eyes, I saw no more wall. I just saw you."

Her laughter transformed into a comfortable grin. She understood now what he looked at in her eyes. Tears rolled down her cheeks, happy tears, tears that were glowing. He was right. She had forgotten who she was, and how to let go and really laugh. She was not destined to live in the shadow of some wall she, herself, constructed. She was destined to laugh and smile. He looked down at her with a nod of approval.

"Some believe it is only with great power that we can hold the evil in check. But that is not what I have found. I have found that it is the small, everyday deeds of ordinary folks that keep the darkness at bay. Small acts of kindness and love," he said, her progress becoming more apparent to him.

"That's beautiful," she said, wiping her face.

"I wish I could say that was mine, but I stole it from Gandalf from the Hobbit."

This made her laugh even harder, to the point that she grabbed her stomach and fell to the side. He rolled his eyes and chuckled to himself while he walked away from her teasing.

"I forgot how nerdy you are," she spat out. She tried to control her laughter and was eventually able to stand to her feet to catch her breath. "I miss it. I really do," she said with genuine feeling.

He kicked a rock to the side and walked to the edge of the cliff overlooking the canyon.

"After this, you'll have to do without it forever I suppose."

Her smile immediately vanished. This was the first time it had really struck her that he was gone, he was really gone. She knew he said he was dead, but she was so caught up in their conversation and reminiscing that she hadn't fully comprehended it. He was dead. He was gone... forever.

7

She didn't want to think about it. She didn't want to think that the person who had been her best friend—even years ago—was gone forever. Sure, they hadn't spoken in quite a while, and yes, their relationship had ended in fire and brimstone. But, that didn't change the fact that they had been incredibly close and had significantly impacted each other's lives. It was like a tease now. He came back for the afternoon to save her and then desert her? It felt disheartening. Although, she surmised, it was probably akin to what he felt all those years ago when she told him she could no longer have any kind of relationship with him.

"You're not going to like the way this story ends," he said, still facing away from her and looking out over the canyon. He took a deep breath and turned from the edge of the cliff. Sauntering over to a nearby bush, he began mindlessly plucking small berries off it.

"I didn't like the way the story started, so I don't see it getting much worse," she sighed.

"You feel good right now, don't you?" he asked, flicking the berries from his palm at the rocks next to him.

"I feel...um, content, I guess," she replied, having to think about it for a few seconds. Yes, she was content. She had made miles' worth of progress today.

"Haven't felt suicidal today, right?" he said, tossing a berry on the ground. Staring at him, she tried to figure out where he was going with this. Knowing him, he would throw a curve ball in there somewhere and she would be taken off guard.

"What's your point?" she asked blatantly. She didn't want to run around in circles until she was hit with some major question that would give her an existential crisis.

"Well, my next question relies on you being of pretty sound mind. I'd hate to get a biased answer," he told her. His tone and word choice sounded like he was about to ask something offensive or controversial. She braced herself.

"I'm not constantly suicidal. I think about it a lot, but it's not like I'm going to get a sudden urge to just do it," she replied, already mounting her defense.

"Isn't that terrifying in itself, though? How it just sneaks up on you?" he said with caution. She shook her head and walked back to her bag, still doing her best to forget that this would be the last time she would ever see him.

"Listen, I hate this. I love you and hate that you're gone. I just can't do this anymore. You've helped me a lot today and I can't thank you enough. But I can't do this knowing that I'll never see you again," she said, packing up her backpack.

"Do you want to be better?" he asked under his breath, as he crushed a berry on the ground under his foot. The juice from the berry spilled onto the rock like his blood once had. She picked up her half-empty bottle of water and took a quick swig. She was interested in the things he said but didn't see an end to the conversation any time soon. They had already been around in circles. If she was going to lose him again, she wanted to do it fast—like ripping off a band-aid.

"What do you mean by that? Of course I want to be better," she said, sighing and zipping up her backpack. He could tell that she was getting irritated and was about to act on that emotion by leaving. It was time to stop relenting. He knew things about her she didn't even know about herself. It was time to face this head on.

"Do you? Can you tell me that you haven't found a sense of comfort knowing that there is an out?" he pressed on.

She was generally a peaceful person who wasn't driven to anger easily, but this made her hands ball into fists. Just a few minutes before, they laughed about the past, and just like his old self, he had to ruin it with a manipulative question. Paired with the fact that this was coming from a man she once loved and would never see again, she didn't know whether to feel sadness or hatred. He was ripping away curtain after curtain that she had forgotten were even there, revealing things she never wanted to see.

"Everyone likes to believe that they want to be better, but few will actually put in the work to be better. Why do you think that is?" he asked, focused on crushing another berry with his boot rather than making eye contact with her. Hearing his condescending tone, she silently despised him in that moment. He always thought that he was so smart and she was just an ignorant little girl. Why couldn't they just live with the memories they had and laugh like they had a few minutes before? Maybe tearing down the wall was too painful and too much work. Why couldn't she just stop this tense and emotional conversation, and go on with her life pretending she was okay? She had been successful up to this point putting on the fake smile, keeping up the fake relationships, and making sure everyone else was helped and happy.

"Yet, it hasn't gotten you anywhere. The fake smile, fake relationships, making sure everyone else is happy. It's only dug a hole deeper into depression."

She snapped.

"SHUT UP! YOU DON'T EVEN KNOW ME ANYMORE! YOU'RE NOTHING! WE WERE BEST FRIENDS FOR MAYBE A YEAR AT MOST AND THAT WAS IT!"

Remaining calm, he sat on the ground looking at the smooth stone beneath him. He took a slow breath in, then exhaled fully. She waited for his response as he continued to inhale and exhale deeply and deliberately. She loomed over him, thinking she finally had the upper hand, but then saw in his face that he had full control. She was the one who had lost it. After a few moments of nothing but his audible breaths, he stood up to her level. She stepped back, not in fear of him, but in unconscious reverence for the person in charge of the situation. She had relinquished all power the moment she cracked. He had flung the last curtain open and revealed her true self and the path she had been walking down most of her life. He strode over to the rocks that held the blood stain.

"This," he said, gesturing toward the blood, "is what your fake smile and fake relationships get you in the end. They lead to death. You need to heal yourself before you can help others."

He walked away from the stain and sat back down, his back now turned against her. Still in a state of anger and shock, she glanced at the blood once again. The first time she had seen it, her heart was broken for her friend's pain and tragic end. Now she looked at it in fear of what she was becoming. Is this how it would end if she didn't change? Did she want to be better?

8

I pulled into the canyon parking lot at an old, familiar spot. Turning down my music, I could see that most everything was the same. It looked like maybe a few more people than usual had been there, but other than that, it was still our spot. I remembered when I saw it for the first time. It looked like nothing special. In fact, she and I were in a bit of an argument that had been boiling on the way there and we weren't really talking by the time we arrived. That was our relationship, though. No matter what dark path our discussions took us on, we'd recover and still stand by each other's side—another reason to feel hurt when she no longer wanted to stand by me.

I looked to the empty passenger seat next to me. Closing my eyes, I imagined her sitting with me, smiling at the prospect of a new adventure on the horizon. I would often hold her knee as I drove along to the particular spot. I reached out to grab it, but my hand only touched the leather of the seat. I opened my eyes and was reminded that I was alone.

I stepped out of my vehicle and popped the trunk, grabbing my backpack. It was the same backpack I used when we were together, and just like me, it hadn't changed one bit except for looking a little more tired and worn. Unlike the backpack, though, I eventually snowballed into a tangled mess. A man with a gun whose only intent was to end his own life.

I remembered my first time on the trail. I watched as she grabbed her things from the trunk, excited for what was to come. I remember I trudged around, slowly grabbing my gear, only thinking about going home and never seeing this place again. Our fight had affected my entire outlook and mood that day and all I wanted to do was curl up at home and ignore her. She wouldn't let that happen.

Today as I stepped onto the trail, I felt an overwhelming sense of nostalgia as I walked past trees and bushes. It's not that I remembered every specific thing, but I felt a sense of belonging as I continued down the trail—a belonging that could only be matched by one thing; being next to her. My thoughts dwelled on her a lot today but that didn't bother me much. I was going to be dead either way. Better to keep myself in that downward mindset so that I wouldn't change my overthinking mind. Besides, I chose the site of the canyon for the memories. That, and knowing once I got to the top of the cliff, I wouldn't want to come back down. Just another reason to make sure I'd go through with it.

We always measured the difficulty of a hike by how hard it was to come back down from the trail. If it was just as tricky coming down as climbing up, then it was a difficult hike. Those were our favorites. There were many different paths we hiked, but this one was where we made the most memories. It was practically untouched by other people. There was the small pond along the way where we had often spent an afternoon relaxing and letting the world melt away. One day at the pond was particularly upsetting for her. It was the anniversary of her mother's death. She never spoke about it to me, reserving those feelings only for her and her therapist. I was never quite sure why she didn't share any of it, except for the fact that it was possibly too painful to talk about. Probably too difficult to talk about her aunt needing to raise her because of her horrible father.

Any time she texted me and said she needed to be "relieved," I knew it was something dark relating to her family and that she needed to be taken away somewhere. One of those places was the pond. The first time we saw it, little did we know that it would become a safe haven and escape from her unpleasant memories.

After the pond came the part where we ventured off trail. It started with me pointing out a small crevice on the side of the canyon about halfway up. It was a difficult climb, but I was determined to see if there was anything interesting at the top. Plus, I was always looking for ways to impress the pretty girl beside me. I grabbed onto the rough edges and hoisted myself up, rock after rock. The fresh air had helped the tension of our argument dissipate, and she chuckled at the sight of me struggling to get to that spot that was more than likely nothing at all. I was going to make it, though. I wanted our first trip there to have better memories than just the spat on the ride up.

I stepped onto the solid rock and brought myself to see what the dark crevice was. It was indeed a small opening that could be a cave. Finding caves at this canyon wasn't anything unusual. They were plentiful in this area, and most went back a few yards before ending in a giant rock wall. I yelled down to her that I would be right back, and plopped onto my stomach to crawl into the cave—an act my mother would have actively protested against since snakes often hide in these places to get a brief respite from the hot sun. Being the young rebellious man that I was, I went on with the adventure, figuring that encountering a snake was worth the risk to pursue the mystery.

As I scooted my stomach across the dirt, the light slowly vanished and the cave opened up to where I could stand. When I realized that it went even further back, I quickly crawled back out and coaxed her to join me. We both wriggled in and stood up into the darkness. We pulled out our phone flashlights and saw that the cave was much deeper than we had thought, and our hearts beat quicker at the prospect of discovering something no one had before. We continued on until a small beam of light cut through the darkness and we saw an opening. Rushing toward it, we both looked up the side of the cave to where the aperture was. Certainly a difficult climb, but we were not going to stop there. I hoisted her up first, and then she helped pull me up. We initially saw nothing much, aside from some trees and bushes, but after making our way through the brush, we stumbled upon our Narnia. It was a small, abandoned cabin sitting in the middle of an overgrown field.

Giddy with anticipation, we carefully turned the rusty knob and the door creaked as it swung open. Among the dust and stagnant air, we found a small kitchen with old pots and pans, a small sitting area and a bed frame with no mattress. This would become our special escape. It was where we danced together for the first time. She hadn't known how, so she stood on my feet as I twirled her around the cabin until we collapsed in laughter. Sweet memories and long nights were spent there, believing that nothing could ever take our Narnia away. I was wrong. She could take it away, and she did.

I stood staring at the abandoned cabin one last time. A tear rolled down my cheek, knowing there would be no more memories made there. After a few months of spending weekends at the cabin, she noticed another spot she wanted us to explore. This spot was my end goal today. The spot she wanted me to see would become the last spot I would stand alive.

I remember the day she discovered it. We had just finished lunch. She was energized and I wanted to sleep. She jumped from the cabin's deck and rushed to the side of the canyon to the flat land above us. I never noticed it before but it was covered in large boulders. If you took each one separately and slowly, you could leap to the top of the canyon. So she did. I sat and laughed as I realized how much she resembled a frog as she leaped. She could hear me laughing, and a smile broke out on her face as she climbed, eventually making it to the top. I didn't expect her to find anything until she called for me to join her at there. As I leaped all of the boulders and stepped onto the flat land above the canyon, I saw her standing on the edge of the cliff staring at the horizon. I walked towards her, passing a few boulders and bushes, before arriving at the spot where I could see the entire canyon. Color and light flooded my eyes and I was met with a sense of accomplishment. This spot was ours. The place where our best memories would be made. Memories were all I had now, as I stepped once again onto the flat land above the cabin.

I took a deep breath, feeling my chest rise and fall. My mind had never felt more lucid or alert. Once I made it to that point, the memories faded away and my mission was clear. Knowing full well that my own demise awaited me at the end of the cliff, I stepped forward and readied myself to explore and experience what exactly happens to the body and mind upon death.

I suddenly felt nervous about being alone. I wondered again about what I had written in my note. Why did nobody want to hike with me? Or even just hang out with me? Why did nobody talk to me? I saw people post on Facebook constantly about their amazing lives and all their friends and family. Nobody wants to share the reality of life, and that it ends. Nobody wants to share that they, those friends and those family members, have problems of their own. No, we put our best mask on and plaster it all over the internet for people to compare their lives to. If our lives don't measure up to those standards, then we toss ourselves aside like we're not worthy of...of what? Them? That's exactly right. All of them.

I continued onward to the edge. I pulled out my phone and

saw my signal reignite. We had thought we were in heaven when we found out that this was the only spot that held a signal. It was heaven before, but I was about to make it hell as I plodded step after step toward my end goal.

I didn't think much about my funeral. I thought more about how long it would take them to find me. My parents knew I went to the canyon often, but never knew about this spot. I guessed they would probably find my car and then she would get involved and know the spot to find me. How long until they would notice I was missing? My guess would probably be a week since no one contacted me unless I did so first. It would only be because of work, too. After my absence from work, they'd ask around and one thing would lead to another.

I remember feeling everything felt like I was in slow motion. Then, I saw the horizon.

9

She screamed into the open canyon echoing throughout, letting her knees hit the ground. In the distance, birds took flight to the sudden exclamation as her chest pounded wildly. The exhaustion was pushing her to the edge. He turned to see her and knew that she was struggling. The war inside her head was waging and she was barely making progress, but she was making some. This was her battlefield and the fact that she was fighting was proof that she was striving for something better than what she was. He knew her energy was depleted, but she still pushed forward. He knew that so many people became complacent living with their depression and anxiety, accepting it as their lot in life. They could easily set aside their best selves for the never ending cycle that promised continued misery, but still the comfort of the familiar. And the relief of knowing that there was a quick way out if they needed it.

Some would even joke about wanting to die and how terrible their lives were, but never made any effort to progress or to eliminate those feelings. They lived with the nagging but consoling thought of ending it all. One late night was all it would take. One late night when they would see only the endless day in and day out cycle ahead of them, inching closer and closer to an undesirable end. We all wondered why the suicide rates were so high. They need help right? They need someone to talk to. They need to figure out these problems and push past them. After all, he often was told that suicide was a permanent solution to a temporary problem. Was it though? What was the temporary problem? A bad break up, loss of a job, a loved one's death—maybe all three concurrently? The intensity of those problems would often pass with time or self-reflection.

Now that he had seen behind death's curtain, he could identify the depression and anxiety that tormented him, and was now tormenting her. She would be eighty-years-old, fighting this same battle she was falling to the ground fighting now. If he could only convince her to put the work in now—though difficult, anguished and painful—she could be well on her way to victory by the next morning. He desperately needed her to heed his words.

In and out, she breathed the warm air. She stared into the soil as the light breeze pushed around some dust in front of her knees. He wanted to help but knew that her crisis was something she would have to deal with on her own terms. He observed her with concern, worried about whether she would be able to make it through. Her future was clouded by her storm, and there was no way he could predict it. He stood up and sympathetically walked toward her.

"I want to be better. I do. I don't know how. Is that why you're here?" she asked him, breathing heavily.

"Yes," he said calmly. He looked down at her pained face. She thought she would feel relief at this revelation, but she did not. Instead, her heart started beating faster and she could feel anxiety creeping into her chest. He bent to his knees, watching her carefully.

"That—that right there is why I know you're telling the truth and want to get better. Do not shy away now. Face it head on."

She questioned his logic as a million thoughts ran through her mind regarding how, exactly, she could overcome this. She had learned from him about her ego, waking up at the same time daily, and creating her own path in life, but she felt like there was still something else lurking in the dark recesses of her mind that she would have to face. As anxiety's icy hand reached out to her, she recalled countless times before when she had taken ahold of it and shut everyone out.

"Your anxiety just got worse. It's fighting back. It knows that you're considering changing paths and it doesn't want you to. You're taking control and now, it has to work harder to keep you in its grips. It doesn't like that."

She felt it shoot through the core of her thoughts as tears ran down her cheeks. They fell to the ground in a steady rhythm from her face that was beet red from both heat and mental exhaustion.

"Don't stop. Don't give up. Let's give you some ammo to fight it and take a step onto the path." he exclaimed, staring at the despair in her eyes. It was chaos inside her head, and she was doing her best to compose herself.

"I just want to be better. How do I fight this? I'm scared!" she spat out, barely holding onto her sanity. She had never shown so much emotion to someone before then. Tears bombarded the ground beneath her, and she desperately tried to not lose herself.

She looked up from the ground and opened her eyes; hoping to be met with a loving embrace from him. But he was gone. Now alone with her own thoughts in the canyon she turned her head looking for him. Was that it? Did it end in the middle of a battle she already felt she had lost? She stepped forward barely an inch and crossed her arms defensively. She quietly stood on the rock of the canyon as the confusion of what was happening pulled back her tears. He was gone, the canyon had grown dark, and now in front of her was a path leading her back to the blood stain.

"Where did you go?" she asked into the quiet of the dark. She felt cold and alone, but oddly content. The path before her was clear. At the end of it she could see the blood stain, and something else, two shiny, black, leather shoes that as her eyes followed up became a figure that stood directly above the blood. It was an attractive, well-dressed man who stared into her eyes. As she stared into his, she could see immediately that it was not her friend. She felt drawn to this man and she could tell by the burning desire in his gaze that he also wanted her. This man had come to see her before. This man is death.

He had no scythe, dark cloak, or skeleton hands. Just the lure of a handsome man her age who clearly wanted her. The path to him was long and the color from the canyon dripped away. She didn't want to experience the path leading to him. She only wanted to be at the end, with him, with death. She only wanted to feel his embrace and escape this terrifying place.

"There's another path," she heard through the howl of wind that had picked up around her. "There's another path!" her friend sat in front of her, screaming. She was hunched over the rock of the canyon, eyes closed, breathing erratically. He couldn't see through to what she saw but could see that she struggled with this vision.

Though he was yelling at her, she heard only a whisper in her mind, and she was forced to take her eyes off death to listen closely.

"There is another path!" he screamed at her again and again, not knowing if anything was getting through. He could tell she was facing the strong pull of death's desire and he would have to force her in a new direction.

"There is another path," she heard again. She frantically looked to disconnect from death's stare. She now understood, everything rushed back to her. There was another path. She saw the darkness of her ego begin to shrink as color slowly pooled back into its place in the canyon. She watched as this handsome well-dressed man melted into an angry, old, decrepit man who stole people from the world. She looked to her right and saw grass growing off the path she stood. She took a single step onto it, and felt it's lush, green warmed her soul.

Suddenly, the rocks shook beneath her. Roots wrapped around her remaining foot trying to hold her on the familiar path. Death breathed in heavily and cracked his neck, determined to keep her there. She realized then that death assumed she could be taken easily. That he had controlled her thoughts for so long that she had no others to turn to, but she had experienced a revelation and was determined to be better.

She tried to focus on the grass. It felt strange and unsafe. Although the other path was cold and colorless, at least it was solid and familiar. The grass was off trail, an uncomfortable diversion. It was wild and unknown. It had no promise of protection, other than trust in herself. She was breaking the cycle and forging her own path.

"What do you do when you're terrified and want to go back?" She asked frantically, as she mentally straddled the two paths. She now knew the danger that would lie ahead off the main path.

"You use discipline and push harder to move forward," he whispered to her.

She looked down at her foot that was covered in roots. She had to reinvent her mindset. She was in control. This was her mind. This was her body. This was her choice. She yanked her remaining foot from the roots and stood tall and firmly in the grass.

"Discipline myself," she repeated over and over, "This is my mind, this is my body, this is my choice. My mind, my body, my choice."

As he heard her whispering these words under her breath, he felt a wave of relief wash over him. He leaned back and sat on the ground, exhausted. She had just won her first battle. She had seen and chosen the new path, but the unknown was going to be terrifying and lonely. Although she had taken the first step toward control, the thought patterns she had reverted to all her life were not going to leave quietly.

He still feared for her. He knew there was still one thing that she would have to face before she could move forward. This one thing would both burn the grass and crush the stone paths into rubble. It would either be the end of her or her new beginning. Yet, he also felt hope. He knew she felt stronger and more disciplined than ever, and wondered if maybe, just maybe, that was enough to equip her for the next obstacle he was about to divulge.

10

She opened her eyes and looked at him. Her breathing slowed. He stood up and walked past her as she sat on her knees still contemplating and feeling what had just happened. She felt freer, breathing deeply out of relief. She had tried something new and she wanted to be better. She pushed herself to the edge. He hoped she could push herself even further still. Yet, her mind rested on how her daily life would change. In theory, making changes and thinking positively sounded achievable, but how would this apply in real world situations?

"You have to change your mindset first," he instructed. "You have to make small steps before you can get to actual life applications. You are stranded in the ocean, but you're already thinking about how to build a shelter once you're on land. You need to focus first on getting *to* land," he said as he rubbed his chin.

She felt like his analogy was decent enough, but also didn't want to become too focused on the swimming, or become too complacent treading water that she wouldn't plan for the bigger steps that needed to come afterward. And when was it time for those steps?

"You will know when," he told her confidently.

How though? At what sign would she know she was ready to move forward?

"You will know because you will ask yourself if you're

ready. If you question it, you're ready," he continued.

She had just made a major step forward, but was she ready for another? As she slowly picked herself up from the ground, she could see in his face that he was avoiding something. He was uneasy. His eyes uncomfortably darted around the canyon. There was something lurking in the shadows that he didn't want to verbalize.

"What is it?" she asked softly.

His anxious demeanor was infectious but she forced herself to remain calm. He took a deep breath and closed his eyes.

"We have to talk about it," he replied tentatively. The breath was sucked from her lungs the moment his words reached her ears. What could he possibly bring up now that would be any worse than what she had already endured? What could he say that would push her even further to the edge? She understood that it would take hard work. She was tearing down walls and taking new paths. What more was there?

He walked past her to the edge of the cliff and sat down with his feet dangling over.

"You know what I'm talking about. It's not a completely repressed memory. It's something you've kept silent about ever since it happened. Something you've held onto tighter and tighter as time has gone on," he said, focusing on his feet as they swung back and forth like a carefree child's. He noted the irony as he prepared himself to broach the subject that had stolen the last sliver of her youthful innocence years before.

She looked at his back and beyond that, the canyon. Her heart beat faster. Her anxiety clawed its way back into her mind. She imagined the grassy path again. She imagined herself staring into the unknown, but started to see her first few steps. Depression and anxiety nipped at her heels, but she realized that she felt just a little bit more in control. Instead of shutting down or getting angry, like she had with so many therapists before, she pushed forward into the darkness.

"My parents...," she said, lowering in dismay.

"It's going to kill you. Not physically, but it will destroy you and bring down everything you know. It will force you into a submission of guilt and build your ego higher still," he pleaded with her.

She didn't understand what he meant, but at this point was accustomed to that. She crossed her arms, readying herself for whatever explanation would come next. She turned around and saw the blood stain on the ground, then followed the dirt to the words he had written earlier that morning. It was the only thing that convinced her that this encounter was real.

She was only ten-years-old when it happened. By that age, she had already been physically and mentally scarred. She constantly felt like she had done something fundamentally wrong by just being born. She had learned to choose between hiding in the darkness of her closet while Daddy beat Mommy, or going out there and feeling the blows herself. Daddy would often come home drunk and take his anger out on both of them, blaming them for his life being "wasted away." He could have done something with his life, but instead was stuck coming home to raise his "stupid, bitch daughter." People often asked her why she never told another adult what her dad was doing. Why didn't she try to get help? She tried to rationalize why her brain wouldn't ever tell anyone; it was because she was ten, and that was her daddy. No matter how terribly he tormented and abused them, he was hers, and he was all she knew.

That night, her mother had just walked in and witnessed

him forcefully grab her tiny arm. Mommy always tried to stand between them to take the brunt of the savage abuse. As her mother lunged in to protect her, he turned around with a backhand that forced her to the cold kitchen floor. As usual, in contrast to a light bruise on her own arm, Mommy would have bloody lips and a busted-up face to show her obedience to evil.

He continued pounding his fists on her even as she tried to pull herself up, but something was different this time. Daddy was hitting Mommy harder and harder, and not even letting up to take a drink. He never stopped to scream for her to fix dinner or yell for her to go to her room where he would rape her. Not this time, this time he was silent. Most people assumed that he was drunker than usual that night, and that's what caused the fatal blow. She knew better though, even at ten-years-old. The difference that night wasn't that he was even more drunk; it was that he was sober.

In an instant, her mother's body fell to the ground one last time. Blood pooled around her mouth and the eyes that used to give her so much love went cold and empty. Her mother was dead.

He had unleashed all of his anger and hate with no desire to hold back. He took her mother's life in front of his little girl's eyes, and he didn't care. He only cared about his own life and that they had taken it away from him. Nothing could be blamed on alcohol. This was intentional.

The monster that committed this evil stood in the room just a few feet away. Staring at the body that only ever loved him, he knew he had done something irreversible. He knew he had done wrong. She could feel the guilt in the room as if it were a living being standing there with them. Immediately, he knelt to the ground holding his head in his hands.

"LOOK WHAT YOU MADE ME DO!" he accused her dead mother, crying out in defense. He screamed at the lifeless body that could no longer hear the torment of his abuse. After a moment of staring at the corpse and slowly coming to the realization of what just transpired, he remembered that he had a daughter standing a few feet away who had just witnessed her own mother's death.

She stood there, innocence shattered, with her bruised arm and tears drying on her face—not completely understanding what had just happened, but still knowing something was very wrong. This is the moment that her therapists believe the incident came to an end. An officer knocked on the door for another noise complaint, and she was taken to her aunt's house where she lived from that point forward. She never spoke of what happened afterward, and it's the reason that she knew, right there on the cliff, that he was telling the truth.

"Mommy?" the ten-year-old girl called out into the deafening silence. She didn't quite understand what death was, but she now understood what evil was. He turned and stared into his little girl's eyes with panic and desperation.

"That's not me...," he opened out his arms to her as he slowly got up from the ground. He stepped toward her and she stepped back in fear, holding her bruised arm.

"Honey, that's not me," he repeated, trying to comfort her. But, she knew who he was. No amount of remorse or pleading was going to change her mind. He kept stepping toward her and she kept retreating. At that moment, unbeknownst to her, the foundation of her proverbial path began its construction.

"Goddamn it, THAT'S NOT ME!" he yelled at her with anger and panic. Suddenly, there was a knock at the door. His head turned and his adrenaline spiked. An officer asked for her daddy to open the door. From there, everything went blurry except those words indelibly etched in her mind. *That's not me.* For years following the incident, she would go to sleep at night and see her daddy creeping toward her with his arms open wide saying, "That's not me." She shuddered at the mere thought.

She looked down where he had sketched those words in the dirt. No one knew about that interaction. She had never talked about it. It was too eerie—too traumatic to verbalize. She planned on taking it to her grave. It was a scar from that night that wouldn't heal.

That's not me.

11

"I held off bringing that memory up because I didn't know how you would react to it," he told her, standing on the edge of the cliff brushing dust off of his clothes.

She looked at the words written on the ground. She hadn't been broken up at all by them. He had used them to prove to her that the situation she was in was real. She had gone through many therapy sessions which had helped tremendously with her past. She remembered the biggest breakthrough was coming to terms with forgiving the ten-year-old girl who did nothing.

The weight on her shoulders left from that day was lifted, and she felt a calming peace with herself. The peace she felt today didn't take away the suicidal thoughts festering within her, but she never made the connection. Her dad had died in prison years ago. That part of her life was over. It was done. So, why bring it up?

"It's a part of you that's still smoldering. You've found peace, and I can't tell you enough how wonderful that discovery is but, that's not the end of the story." He held his water bottle close to his chest, and was getting anxious again. She didn't like seeing him anxious. What was causing the sudden rise in uneasiness? The story had ended for her dad a long time ago. She was moving on with her life. She couldn't be dragged back into these memories.

"You haven't *given* peace yet. You want to put out that burning ember completely. If you smother what's left of the ember then you'll be left in the cold," he said twisting his palms around the bottle as it crackled like a fire slowly burning out. "That's not me" stared at her from the dirt.

She had actually pieced together what he meant by his analogy for a moment. Her raging fire of anger and hatred had been a part of her for most of her life, and it had burned everything. The fuel for the fire was blaming herself for not intervening even though she was only a child. "It should have been me", she would tell herself, and the fire in her heart would burn brighter. Until the day she found out about her father's passing, the fire calmed down over time until the coals just faintly glowed. This dying fire was the peace she had felt, and it was the only thing that mattered to her. She had control of this fire, and it was time to put it out completely. So why did he want her to bring the fire back? It would bring her life crashing down.

"You're right," he looked up from his bottle. "It could do that. It could burn everything you've ever known down to the ground. Putting the fire out or letting it burn everything down aren't the only options though," he said as tears formed in his eyes. His tears were a first for the day. He was stressed and contemplated what he would say next.

"If you're talking about forgiving myself for what happened, I don't know what to tell you. Maybe it's something you can't see, but I already forgave myself. It's over. I've given myself peace," she responded before he could keep speaking, hoping to break down some of the anxiety clearly eating at him.

"I'm not talking about forgiving yourself...," he shook his head looking down. "I'm talking about forgiving him," he whispered looking up at her.

The dying coals reignited in her heart and suddenly a bright fire grew in an instant. She broke eye contact with the words on the ground as they melted away in the rage that would soon consume her. She stared at him, and he could see that she lost herself.

She ran towards him and shoved him to the ground. His head would have hit the cliff, but instead it swung down over the hundred foot drop. His body just barely lay on the edge. As he motionlessly stared at the blue sky above him.

A moment later, he was staring to his right and then just as suddenly to his left. She punched his face as her anger grew realizing the newfound knowledge that he could in fact be touched. Her face contorted, and she gritted her teeth in absolute anger and hatred.

If he had wanted to reignite the fire, he just did. It burned down the grassy path, it crushed the stone path to rubble; it destroyed every path, and clouded her eyes to even seeing death. Everything was gone except for her boiling hatred. He didn't fight back at all. She didn't care or concern herself with his passiveness. Punch after punch, his face became beaten and broken. Blood splattered down the canyon as his head hovered just above the steep drop. She wanted so terribly for his smug face to fall from the cliff edge never to be seen again. If he were still living, he would have been dead by now.

Running out of energy she fell beside him on the ground. She rolled to her back and took heavy breaths. He remained calm as he stood up from the spot and brushed himself off. His face broken, he was unable to see clearly. Blood streamed down his face from a gash over his eye. He dabbed it with his finger. Suddenly, not completely, his eyes began to reshape. The gash restitched as the blood pulled back under his skin. He was slowly healing.

"You're...I could touch you this whole time," she panted out as she stared at the canyon's beautiful blue sky. "I would have kicked your ass a long time ago if I would have known I could touch you," she said pushing herself up off the ground and rising to her feet.

They both stood in silence for a moment. He couldn't help but laugh at her statement. Even she let out a giggle at her joke. For a moment she forgot about his request and about how she was now standing in ash with no path and no goal. She had burned down everything. As he bled, she looked at her knuckles that were also marked with blood. She saw that his face was healing rapidly. Annoyed, she shook her head and started to walk away.

"You can hit me as many times as you want for as long as you want, but this is a conversation we are going to have. It's going to start with me telling you to forgive him every time." Just hearing those words again made her tense. She clenched her fists and hurriedly walked back to him.

"Yeah? Just like that? Forgive the monster that beat my mom to death? Let's just give him a free pass for everything why don't we?" she said getting close to his face still moving and morphing back into place.

"Can you honestly tell me that you're keeping forgiveness from him to teach him a lesson about consequences?" he said rolling his eyes at her. He lightly touched his lip to check for blood, and it felt as though his face was back to normal.

"What? What does that even mean?" she said shoving him again. She could barely hear him over the crackling fire that grew inside her once more. She didn't care about any path. She only cared about ignoring what he was telling her to do.

"You just asked if we should give him a free pass. A free

pass implies the only reason you don't forgive him is because he doesn't deserve it. You imply he has to face his consequences like a child. That's the reason you won't give it to him."

"Obviously, it's deeper than that! It was just a fucking random reason I threw out there!" she yelled back at him.

"Alright then! Let's hear it!" he yelled back motioning his hands away from his chest as if he were a fighter stepping into a ring.

"HE BEAT MY MOTHER IN FRONT OF ME AND KILLED HER!" she screamed stomping her foot down with tears running down her face. Her fists became unclenched.

He quickly wrapped his arms around her and squeezed her into his chest giving her a tight hug. She immediately wept into his shoulder as she felt the burden of hatred and anger wash over her. She felt the fire raging out of control and the chaos it created in herself as she wept into him. "You don't understand. You'll never understand what he did to me: to us," she said as she kept weeping. He held her tightly in his arms.

"You're absolutely right. I will never understand what you went through witnessing the things you've seen," he spoke clearly as he tried to comfort her. Her heart began to calm down and she embraced his loving hug; however, her mental defenses were still on high. He could feel this barrier. "Forgiveness like this isn't easily given out," he said carefully choosing his words. She breathed heavily into his shoulder. "There's a lot of questions that come with it. The obvious one is 'why would he deserve it?' The answer obviously is he doesn't deserve it. Also, if we give him forgiveness then where is your mother's justice? How can he get away free? Where's your justice? What stops him from just doing it again and again until more people are dead in the ground?" She didn't like what she was hearing and almost decided to leave his embrace. She couldn't though. He didn't force her to remain, but she desperately needed someone to hold.

"It makes sense to loathe him and act this way. Your anger is not wrong. Every single fiber of your being is not wrong. The fire that burned bright and took everything down is not evil. It is not the work of death or the work of depression or anxiety. It's not even anger. It's passion. It's your drive. I don't blame you. You don't blame yourself anymore. No one blames you. The way you hate him and loathe him is valid." Her thoughts were becoming more collected as she removed her face from his shirt. He had just told her that she was right. Something she never expected.

"It is valid," she whispered. He released his arms, and she backed away from him slowly. She had just been validated by someone who had killed himself.

No more paths. The validation was it. It was the moment she knew she couldn't continue because there was nowhere to continue. She had to leave. She walked back to her backpack and picked it up putting it across her back.

He watched her, unable to speak up or stop her. This was the moment of life and death and she wasn't even aware of its significance. Everything was in her hands. She could either look past the veil or she could leave the canyon holding onto her valid hatred.

She stopped and looked around the canyon. She was confused. The boulders that normally led down to where the cabin was were gone. She looked around closely at the far distance. Everything looked blurry and out of focus. She had never needed glasses. What was going on? She turned to look at him. He had his hands in his pockets. He grinned and looked up at her.

"Did you figure it out?"

12

"What are you talking about? Where are the boulders? The cabin?" she asked confused, staring at him. Her eyes quickly darted around her surroundings as she became less and less familiar with where she was exactly. The only recognizable part was the cliff that overlooked everything. Even then, the distant rolling hills and wilderness seemed lost to her. It was as if she was standing in a canyon she had never been to, but at the same time she felt right at home.

Had it been like this all morning? She couldn't even remember seeing the lake or the cabin. She remembered setting her backpack down, and she remembered him making that horrid statement. It was as if the memories of them laughing together as they hiked had been a distant dream, and now she was slowly waking up.

"You didn't figure it out then," he said walking slowly toward her. She wouldn't let herself fall into anger but she felt worried about what was happening and stepped back from him cautiously. The warm air quickly melted away into a cool breeze as she felt clouds above her start to form.

"Figure? Figure what out?" she asked hesitantly. His demeanor was changing as was the sky above her. What was this? Why was everything, including nature, seemingly acting together in concert as if part of a synchronized dance?

"You're not going to like it, but I hope that you've learned enough and are able to understand," he spoke. She stopped moving as her feet just touched where the ground had disappeared into a blurry hue moments ago. He met her and took her backpack off for her setting it on the ground. So confused by what was happening around her, she didn't think twice about it. She was thinking about their previous conversation. How he had validated her in the way she felt and how she had won at least the final conversation. It was over. There couldn't be another bombshell.

"What is it?" she asked trembling.

The way he spoke made her think that he was about to undo everything she thought they had resolved. If this whole meeting were a sham, then everything could be washed away, and everything could have been a lie.

He looked up to the sky and watched the clouds start to form above them. Would she be right where she started again because of her stubbornness to hold onto hatred? She looked at him hoping for some kind of answer to her inquiry. Why wasn't he answering her? She needed his help. Couldn't he see that?

He continued looking up at the sky wondering when the first raindrops would fall. Her heart started to beat faster, and she could feel her worry turn into something greater. She began fueling her anger and hatred more. The fire started inside her as she looked at him. He was supposed to help her, but instead he was ignoring her.

In that moment, she stood on the edge of falling into the trap she had known all her life. While looking at him, the familiar touch of overthinking began again without giving her the faintest clue as to what was happening around her. A new thought entered her mind. She had never had it before—a thought that didn't take sides—not of hatred nor forgiveness, but her own thought. It was not a feeling but a thought. The thought had been planted hours before, and now sprouted from the ground that once held a forest. The same forest she had burned down with her hatred.

She realized that regardless of what was happening, or what he revealed, it didn't matter. She knew her path now. There was no wild forest, no uncontrolled storm, no walls, just her. She would walk her path. She would begin her discipline today. She started tearing down her ego in that moment. She started building herself up in that moment. She would invent herself today, and if the time ever came, she now had the tools to reinvent herself.

He could never undo the conversation they just had, even if he came out laughing proclaiming it all a big joke to watch her suffer. She would control her emotions and choose her reactions. He could stand there looking up at the clouds in silence forever and disappear without telling her anything. It didn't matter, her life was her life. She would make her own decisions. She would not be controlled by anyone, and she would make herself be the best she could be. She would raise every aspect of her life to meet her expectations and she would be the strong woman she believed she could be.

She stopped looking at him and looked up at the clouds beginning to form, and grinned. She felt right. As she stepped through the field of the scorched thoughts in her mind she saw new plants begin to grow. There were no paths except for the ones she chose to walk upon. Growing from that first thought that she was going to be okay, she came to realize what she was being taught.

Her dad still controlled her emotions. Her dad still controlled her with the clouds, the walls, the fires, and the thorns that she had known and had buried deep inside for most of her life. Her dad was the monster that killed her mother and she had given him the chains that wrapped around her feet, causing her to stumble.

She stopped looking at the clouds and looked into the eyes of a man who had supported her and helped her so much that day. A smile split across each of their faces. She wasn't only taking away the chains from her father who had controlled her, she was breaking the chains so that no one could ever control her. She was forgiving the man who had murdered her mother right in front of her eyes years ago. She looked at her best friend and he looked back smiling.

"That's not me," she told him with a cry of happiness in her throat.

Tears filled his eyes as she let go of the man to whom she gave forgiveness. She let out a small laugh. She couldn't help it.

The storm that had had been building inside her head was dissipating. This scorching fire that burned everything down didn't go out but it kept her warm. The wall of suicidal thoughts was disappearing. Her chains were broken, and she was free to choose a new and bright path.

Life would get worse. Fires would burn again. Walls would come back, and storms would rage stronger still. There would be times when she would feel like a razor would be her only option. She would fail and fail again.

However, she didn't accept that path. She wouldn't stare at that razor and see that path as the only one. She would reinvent herself and push herself to discover that the journey on her path was more important than the end of her path. She would build self-discipline. She would control her ego. She would control the battle and win the war. Death would inevitably meet her one day. She would stare it face to face, not out of submission to its will but as a continuation of the path she would choose to take.

13

For the first time on top of the cliff, he felt a sense of gratitude. He could see how she had grown from a woman secretly holding onto her past and keeping all of her depression and anxiety locked up into a woman facing herself and pushing forward. Not only that, she now saw that she could be better, and she saw the struggle that she would have to face each day. She didn't shy away from this opposition. Life could get worse for her, much worse; however, she would be that much better.

In the abandoned conversation a question still remained floating around waiting for its equal answer. What was she supposed to have figured out? She started trying to guess the twist as if she were watching an M. Night Shyamalan movie. Was she really dead? Maybe he was actually God? Maybe it was all just a dream created for her to save herself? The verdict was up in the air, and she felt nowhere close to finding the answer. Why were the clouds currently storming above her, and why was she not seeing the cabin past the surrounding boulders? Why was everything blurry in the distance? As she stood next to him, a light breeze picked up.

"I don't know what you're about to tell me," she said with confidence. He smiled at her.

With her newfound perception, he knew that no matter what he revealed to her at this point, she would receive it with a new sense of understanding. They would begin a new conversation, and hopefully he would see a side of her he had always hoped to see.

"I came here to help you. I never came here to hurt you," he said looking at the clouds that were becoming increasingly more dangerous with every passing moment. He wondered if this development hinted at her upcoming revelation. Would she react poorly, and would the events of the day all have been for nothing?

She looked at him with confusion as he thought to himself. She didn't care for the drawn out anticipation she was feeling. Whatever the revelation was, it greatly concerned him. His concern seemed greater than before when he brought up her parents.

"Nothing you can say will take me away from the new life I'm starting," she said confidently. He lowered his head not looking at her. He knew that she would notice. The entire time they were up on the cliff, he had been at least able to look her in the eyes. Not now, knowing what he had to confess. Seeing his eyes dart down away from hers caused an unwavering sense of concern in her chest.

This new conversation wasn't completely about her she realized. Up until this point, everything on the cliff had been about her growth and how she was going to get better. This moment was different. This moment was about him and his actions. What had he done?

He walked around her to where the blood stained the ground. Bending down, he held his chin to examine the stain. Almost as if the chess board had magically reappeared, he planned out his next move, wary and ignorant of her reaction to his words. She had to be able to figure it out. She could figure it out if she looked closely. It was right there for her to see the whole time. She just had never been close enough to really look.

Without his guidance, it easily passed her by.

"Look at this closer," he gestured at the stain. Obliging his request, she walked to where he was bending down. She knelt down next to him and jokingly held her chin also mimicking him as she tried to lighten the mood in any way possible.

He kept his eyes on the stain. She hadn't been this close to it before and saw no reason to look at it now. A blood splatter is a blood splatter. She straightened herself up and looked at it with more intensity, looking for...she didn't know exactly what.

Upon closer inspection, she did see something different with the stain. There was something awkward about the shape and the consistency of the color. The shape was a giant oval. She had always assumed that it was from the spreading of the blood when he shot himself. He would have been on one side of the stain and boom! The blood would've sprayed across the ground.

As she looked at it now, she could see that it wasn't that simple. The blood should have spread more as a cone outwardly spraying with dark red on one end and light red on the other— especially if it were a gun shot. This stain; however, had two dark red spots on the perimeter of the oval and lighter discoloration in the middle. It was as if the blood had flowed from the outside in. This stain wasn't from a gunshot wound. Her eyes widened. This stain came from cut wrists.

She fell backwards onto the ground and quickly pushed herself away, still staring at the stain. Her eyes filled with tears, and fear engulfed her entire body.

"Am I dead?!" she yelled at him.

The razor flashed in her mind as she remembered how it felt when she saw it in her backpack and dropped it to the ground. At that point, she had been shown how to progress and be a better person. Now, her entire world was crashing down as she stared at where she had possibly died. Being dead would explain why she didn't remember anything.

Was she already dead? Was he there to tell her that it was too late? Was he death? Was he escorting her to hell? Had the whole purpose been to bring her crashing down? He turned to her and held out his hands in an effort to calm her down.

"Breathe. Calm down. It's okay. Just breathe," he said in a soothing voice. She pushed herself away from him still staring at the stain. She had definitely figured something out, but he would have to fill in the blanks. Her eyes snapped at him as she tightly gripped the dirt. As tears of panic streamed from her eyes, she tried to rationalize any possible outcome.

"You're not dead. I promise. You're very much alive," he said hoping to put a stop to any thoughts of permanence. She looked back again to the stain. She couldn't stop staring at it. Its dark tint haunted her now that she thought it might be her own blood.

He had said she wasn't dead, then what was this stain? Was this the place where someone else had died? Her breathing slowed gradually, and she regained a little composure. Even so, she desperately tried to figure out what was happening..

He had lied initially, so could she trust him now? Looking at the stain, there was no doubt that it was where wrists had been cut. At first glance anyone would think it was just a large splatter of blood but the details indicated differently. The stain was clearly from a slow bleed that had pooled underneath the person who had sat there. The questions then multiplied, but one stood out among the rest. Who's blood was this? As her memory flooded back, it felt like a dam was breaking.

She had climbed to the top of the cliff late one night. The only reason she had for climbing the cliff was that she wanted to feel something again. She had packed the razor to see what it would feel like to carry it. She never planned to do anything with it. Then, she remembered sitting next to the bush. She had not wanted to sit on the edge of the cliff being reminded of a time when she was happy. She had felt the high again and the nostalgia that came with that feeling. The guilt she felt had melted away with fond memories. The next thing she remembered, she was being carried on someone's shoulder.

"I'm gonna get you help! Hang in there!" the bolstering man's voice echoed in her head. Then she remembered the flashing lights of red and blue from an ambulance as cops and EMT personnel rushed around. She had seen the bandages around her arms in the ambulance. She remembered nothing else.

Until the blaring sound of a ring. Her phone screamed at her as she received a call from a long lost friend. She remembered starting the drive to the canyon to have a long conversation that would change her life.

Breathing heavily, she looked at him standing up from the blood stain. There was no question in her mind, this was her blood.

"This is where I killed myself."

14

Emotions and thoughts battled as she sat staring at what was apparently her own blood on the stone. She could see all the different thoughts in her mind running wild and she couldn't even see a clear path. Only chaos existed in her head, she didn't know which way to turn. Fire shot into the air as her anger burned everything, and her rage thrived. Walls stacked high in front of her soul to block any thought of sanity from entering, and the storm surged wildly with fierce lightning that created wildfires burning her mind down. Through the chaos, she saw death staring into her eyes inches from away from her face.

"This is where you *tried* to kill yourself," he corrected. The words he said evaporated as they hit her ears. Even still, trying to kill herself was something she had no recollection of. Her focus shifted to the fact that he had lied to her. He hadn't just lied to *her*; he had lied to her about herself.

Who was he? How had she left the hospital and come to this place? Was any part of this day even real? He had put her through all of this agony, and she already had attempted suicide. Fuck him. How could he have talked to her this entire time knowing that she had already jumped off the edge of insanity before? She should just finish the job, right?

She remembered what she said about not giving in no matter what he had told her. She had not expected this revelation. She had not expected for her world literally to be flipped upside down. She realized now that the world she was seeing wasn't even real. There it was though, the recognition of her real self for the first time in her life.

She saw the walls. She saw the storms. She felt the fires. The battle grew larger and larger. She could feel it. Her face twitched as she contemplated this new reality. What was she going to do? Which side should she choose in the battle over her mind? Should she respond with kindness and understanding? Or should she respond with hatred and loathing? Should she storm off and let the fire consume her? Maybe she should just jump off the cliff since apparently she didn't know if it were real or not.

She didn't decide on any of these options as they flitted through her mind. One by one she passed them by until finally she chose for herself. She controlled her mind. She wasn't going to sway this time. She wasn't picking any of those destructive thoughts, and *she* would decide her reaction.

The fire relaxed to a small roar as a controlled passion she could direct. The storm silenced in her presence. The walls disappeared, and she saw clearly for the first time ever in the face of adversity. Finally she remembered death staring her down. She calmly ignored the beast and focused on the present.

She stood up confidently from the ground. He had not seen this belief in herself until this moment—a confidence that demanded the silence of anyone around. He could feel the shift of power as she thought long and hard about what she was going to say next. The clouds whirled above them. She knew who she was, and she knew what she wanted.

"None of this is real," she stated. The change in her voice became immediately apparent. She showed no fear or anger. She demonstrated a conviction to find out everything she wanted to know.

She stared into him and saw through his charade. For the first time, being with her in this place, he did not know where her mind was going. He did not know if she would explode or if she would respond with empathy. He was now open to telling her *everything* because of the authority that glowed from her being.

"Not in the sense that it is tangible and would be considered real by society's standards. Technically, this place would be a dream to most people." She hated his answer but quickly shut down the emotion. It definitely didn't feel like a dream. She slowly turned around and looked at the environment. Everything felt real.

She could hear the distant sound of nature, the whirling winds that brought together a building storm, and she could see the cliff of the canyon overlooking the darkening horizon. Everything was real to her. Everything was perfect and too elaborate for it to have just been a dream.

"So, you're just a part of my imagination? You never died?" she shot back at him with fierceness remembering that he had lied and deceived her. She was not kind, but she was not cruel. She was exactly what she needed to be. He gave her a look of ignorance.

"It's tricky to say actually," he answered knowing she wouldn't accept his answer. She locked eyes with him like a lioness about to pounce.

"Make it not tricky," she commanded. Her voice was full of strength and meaning. He gently nodded his head as he yielded the authority he once had.

"I don't know myself, actually. I don't know if I'm a visitor from God. I know that this place is incredibly elaborate for a dream. Even though I can feel and think like I'm real, I know

I'm not. I'm not something that belongs in the real world. I remember having the gun against my head, then I woke up in front of my parents' house with my phone. I knew exactly what to do. Like a pre-written script, the knowledge was already in my head. I knew from the beginning that I was here only to help you and that this was a vision inside your head. I know that you're in a coma right now in the hospital. I have no idea where I am or if I actually killed myself or not. Yes, I'm terrified. I can't tell you what happens after death because I honestly don't know what is after death. All I can tell you is that you are alive. You tried to bleed out but had no success. The cabin you mentioned earlier? That cabin was purchased by some rich doctor recently. He came out to look at his new cabin and found you lying right there," he gestured to the blood stain.

She lowered her head as he spoke. She was in a coma in the hospital right now. These events were all in her mind. It felt too real to be made up by her mind though. There he was too, as if he was his own living being, but apparently was just a figment in her subconscious. It would explain why he knew everything about her. It would explain why he could read her mind. It would explain everything. Was he even fearful of death? Maybe she had just projected her own feelings onto somebody else? She closed her eyes and lifted her head again turning around so that her back was to him.

It didn't matter. She felt relaxed and calm. She was in control, yet she didn't feel controlling. She had a passion and conviction, but she did not let either fuel her anger and hatred. She was alive and that in itself was amazing.

"So, why not just tell me that from the beginning? Why any of this?" she asked with a general curiosity. He grinned and watched her as a light sprinkle started to fall from the sky.

"Do you really think you were in a place to actually listen? If I had told you from the beginning that you tried to kill yourself, wouldn't you have just gone and finished the job? I knew I had to ease you into a place where you could accept the truth. So I changed the story." She smiled as she lifted her arms to the rain now falling from the sky. She could feel it running down her arms. She opened her eyes. She looked at her outstretched arms as the rain rolled across revealing the scars she had from the suicide attempt.

Yet, she still smiled. She did not smile because she thought there was any beauty in her scars. No, she found beauty in her breathing. There was beauty in knowing that she was moving forward and that she had taken control of her life. There was beauty in the simple, yet profound, fact that she was alive.

She let out a small laugh in the comfort she was finding. Comfort in the fact that she had become able to smile in the midst of this storm. She felt different. She felt real. She remembered a story her aunt used to tell her of two wolves inside everyone.

One wolf was evil, anger, envy, sorrow, regret, greed, arrogance, and ego. It was the wolf that she had been battling all day. The other wolf was good. He was joy, peace, love, hope, serenity, kindness, and faith. The story continued with the question—which wolf would win the fight? The response was always the same, the wolf that you feed.

She didn't see that response as the end of the story now. It had been a good story keeping her in line by thinking of her actions in the context of life's situations. But now, she only wanted to take the wolves out of the equation completely. She stood feeling the rain as both wolves disappeared from sight. She was alone with her rain. She could see the person she was from the beginning and say,

"That's not me."

15

Taking my time, I made my way to the end of the cliff's edge as the end of my life approached. It was funny to take my time slowly making my way toward death. I started overthinking every action I had taken leading up to the dreadful death that patiently awaited me.

Why was I walking so slowly? What difference did it make if I pulled out my gun and shot myself in the middle of my walk or if I went to the edge of the cliff to sit down and do it? What difference would it make except to make me more comfortable in the end? In the end it's just the end. Death is not some profound action requiring heavy thought, right? It's just an act like any other, right? It's like sex. It's just an act with no hidden meaning other than what people put into it.

The people who come to my funeral would feel the way they do only because they chose to feel that way. Twenty years from now, people, for the most part, will have forgotten about me other than to make the off-handed comment about that guy who had killed himself a while ago. So what does it matter anyway what I do with my life? What does it matter to any of them? I can't keep this facade of living for them. I can't keep this facade of them needing me. I am not needed. I don't need them. I choose to end my life today because there is no getting past the thoughts and storms in my head that have collected.

As I walk, I ponder all of these things. My legs keep moving no matter how many times I think of a good reason to just pull the gun out and end my life instead of making it to the end of the cliff.

On the other side of the boulders surrounding the cliff, I see a small bush, unnoticeable except for the sudden glistening spot on the ground next to it that catches my wandering eye. Let's see what we have here. Why not? I meander toward the bush and examine the ground on the other side of it. There it is, a large red stain on the ground. Probably an animal had been killed here. I find a sort of solace knowing that I will not be the only one who had died upon this cliff; just another splatter of blood. I turn around and march to the edge of the cliff, which is basically the largest boulder on top of the canyon that juts out from the side. I step onto the smooth stone and make it to the edge. I take a deep breath while looking at the beauty of the canyon one last time. I could never truly explain the feelings I would always have standing on the edge of that cliff. The closest I ever came was standing next to her. Yet, she was nowhere to be found.

I was alone with just the harsh metal sitting in my backpack. I take my backpack off and lay it on the ground next to me with a *thunk*.

I unzip my backpack and take out my half empty bottle of water. One last swig I suppose. I didn't have any alcohol so water would have to do. Gulping down the lukewarm water, I clean off my chin where drips had fallen down. I place my now empty bottle of water back into my backpack, and see the tool of my demise staring back at me. This tool is the only thing in my eyesight as my life crumbled around it.

I sit on the ground and touch the pistol's grip. This touch scares me. So many emotions flood me as I'm about to kill myself. None of them matter. I push through and grasp the gun in the palm of my hand, lifting it up. It seems so much heavier than when I loaded it this morning.

"Here's to knowing what's after death," I whisper to myself, lifting the gun to the side of my skull. I don't feel happy or sad. I'm not even thinking about suicide. Yet, here I am, my finger on the trigger.

She lowered her hands to her side turning around to find him looking at her. A familiar gleam she had missed returned to his eyes, and she now saw him once again, a friend. He had given her everything she needed to be better, including this moment when all she needed was to see the warmth and comfort of his gazing hug.

The sprinkle of rain fell slowly on each of their faces. As the rain rolled down her face, she noticed that it rolled down his face as well, taking something with it. As if it were makeup, the rain droplets took the color out of his face. It happened slowly in layers, but she could see that his face was becoming pale.

He wasn't dying. No, he was disappearing into this make believe canyon that felt like home. She felt at home because well, it was her own mind. This place was her mind. The background of the canyon began to flutter in and out of focus in small bursts. She walked to him as the world created in her mind started to fall apart at the conclusion of the beginning of new life.

As the rain took the color out of him, she saw it taking the color out of everything else much more quickly. As it all washed away, the only thing left was an outline of the remnants of what had occurred there. Memories etched into the walls of her mind. No matter, she only cared about the memories that stood in front of her...him. Her eyes filled with tears as his face held onto the bits of color that remained in his life. She could see that he too was beginning to cry. He wasn't crying from joy though. He looked worried.

"I don't know if this is the last time I'm going to see you or not. I don't know if I did it or not. I'm scared," he let out a soft cry.

She grinned at him as her nose and eyes ran like streams down the canyon. It wasn't about their friendship now. It wasn't about the fights they had, and it wasn't about if they had ever really dated or been in love.

This, right now, was about her looking at him as he looked at her. She placed her hand on the back of his head and put his forehead against hers. Not knowing if she would ever see him again felt worse than knowing he was already gone. A sense of hope was given to her that could easily be taken away. She could feel his fear, and she wanted so much to comfort him. This proved difficult as her grin quickly faded and her tears matched his. He projected his fear clearly to her, and she learned one last lesson from him.

It's okay to feel. It's okay to be afraid and not even feel courageous. Moments would come into her life, sometimes, when she would have no control over the situation, and fear would be in her face. She felt his forehead against hers and knew that even if she weren't courageous, she just needed to hold on to the last string of hope that everything would be okay. She smiled up at him, and he smiled back at her.

"I am so proud of you."

The color began draining down his face revealing the pure glowing white underneath. She could see the lines on his face remaining as all of this solidified in her memory. She wept harder as his face froze in time with the last smile he gave her. She was left standing with the knowledge that he would always be with her.

She silently wept and fell to her knees wondering what would happen next as she did her best not to think of what had happened to him. She took a deep breath with her eyes closed.

When she opened her eyes, there she was, lying in a hospital bed with the incessant beeping next to her. She looked down and saw an I.V. running into her arm, and in the distance, her boyfriend slept in a chair. The room slowly came into focus, and she felt her breath return to her. Breathing in, she realized how false the vision had felt. The real world made the vision feel like a distant dream; however, it had been real to her. That was all that mattered. She smiled at the sight of her boyfriend waiting for her. She loved him more than anything and was so happy to see him.

"Ethan...," she breathed out as she gained composure. She saw him slowly wake up, and he realized who was calling his name. His eyes shot open, and he ran to her side, grasping her hand and running his fingers through her hair. She grasped his shoulders holding him tightly.

"I'm here. I've got you. Take it easy. Let me go get the doctor," he said as she held onto him for a few moments not letting go. She just wanted that feeling. She wanted to hold him. She felt his broad shoulders and felt safe in them. Yet something felt different this time. She didn't feel the need to have him next to her, and the oddest feeling was that it felt like she was closer to him because of it. The embrace was her choice. She didn't need him; she chose him.

"You really had us scared, beautiful," Ethan called her. She grinned at the sound of her nickname knowing she probably looked like Frankenstein's monster.

He didn't know the exact words to say, but he knew he wanted to be there for her. She let go of his shoulders, and he started to leave but stopped at seeing her frantically searching for something on the bed. She seemed struck with an urgency to find something.

"What is it?" Ethan asked feeling around the bed with her as she tried to find the mysterious object that seemed so important.

"My phone. I have to check something," she said. Ethan stopped and looked at her with concern.

"I have it. The doctor told me to hang on to it. He was pretty serious. You're not supposed to have it—at least until we know what the root of all of this is," he told her worriedly. She stopped looking for her phone and stared at the foot of the bed.

Ethan might as well have been twiddling his thumbs because he knew that he was coming off as controlling, and before everything that had happened, she would have dropped him with a screaming fit. Ethan anticipated her anger and prepared for the worst but stood his ground not knowing what the root of her suicide attempt was.

She wanted to get mad at him. She wanted to throw a fit. How dare he? It was her phone. Who was he to tell her how she was feeling and what the root of the problem was? She didn't. She felt the raging fire and took control, owning it.

"Ethan, I understand. I really do understand. Can you call a number for me then? You can keep it on speaker phone. It's important. I need to make sure someone I used to know is safe. I just had a terrible dream about him," she said as she stared into his eyes. He was surprised she hadn't torn him apart for taking her phone. He nodded his head in agreement with the compromise and pulled out her phone. As he unlocked it, she told him the number, and he dialed it putting it on speaker. Silently, they both listened. *Ring ring*

I have the gun against the side of my head. My finger is on the trigger with only the horizon to keep me company. Nothing in my body screams for me to do it, but the numbness of apathy tells me it is time. This is it, the make or break moment. I think about the cycle that led me here. I feel the anger and torment I had from the people around me. How incredibly terrible it is that those people would let it get to this point for me. How my own mother and father hadn't even asked "how are you?" in years and how they'll wonder why I did it. The answer would have to be because of them and because of everyone who put on a mask pretending that everything is okay. It is on them. I am just reacting how any person would react. I pushed the gun against my head harder as I feel the intensity of the heat.

Ring ring. She held her breath as the phone rang. It felt like an eternity. The anticipation kept building as she stared at the phone in Ethan's hand. Ethan stood over her not completely understanding the gravity of the situation, but he knew that she needed him there. She couldn't think about if he had already done it or not. She could only wait for the sound of his voice.

I feel something in my pocket. I hear a familiar ring muffled by the cloth separating the air and the speaker, the jingle I had heard every twenty four hours for my entire life, but today I heard it at another place and at another time. I was so focused on what was happening in my head that I forgot I had even brought my phone with me. Not that it mattered. Nobody would ever have contacted me. In fact, I immediately assume it is a notification from a random app or a game I forgot I had downloaded. I reach down to hit silent but there it is again, the jingle. It is a call; not a useless notification. I reach into my pocket and pull out my phone while still holding the pistol with my other hand.

Ring ring. It would only ring one more time, then, nothing. It would be a terribly deafening silence as she braced herself to bawl her eyes out onto her boyfriend's chest. Ethan felt her tension and put his arm around her, holding her closely. Tears began welling up in her eyes.

I looked down at the gun in my hand and then at the phone in my other. I see the name of the person calling me. I place the gun on the ground.

Ethan held the phone in the palm of his hand as she bit her tongue in a last moment of uncertainty.

"Hello?"

She let out a gasp and smiled.